NURSE IN NAPLES

When Nurse Sheila O'Donnell took a post
in an Italian hospital she was dreaming only
of blue skies, warm seas and the romance of
Naples. The reality was a hectically busy,
acute surgical and accident hospital, where
every patient was surrounded by a swarm of
excitable relatives. Unable to speak a word
of Italian, her first weeks on the wards were
hilarious, tearful and at times nearly
catastrophic. Aided and abetted by eleven
kind and fun-loving Irish nuns, she
gradually settled in and developed a deep
affection for this colourful and sunny land.

NURSE IN NAPLES

Nurse In Naples

by

Sheila O'Donnell

Dales Large Print Books
Long Preston, North Yorkshire,
BD23 4ND, England.

British Library Cataloguing in Publication Data.

O'Donnell, Sheila
  Nurse in Naples.

    A catalogue record of this book is
    available from the British Library

    ISBN   1-84262-413-X pbk

First published in Great Britain in 1962 by Robert Hale Limited

Copyright © Sheila O'Donnell 1962

Cover illustration © John Hancock by arrangement with
P.W.A. International Ltd.

The moral right of the author has been asserted

Published in Large Print 2005 by arrangement with
Robert Hale Limited

Dales Large Print is an imprint of Library Magna Books Ltd.

Printed and bound in Great Britain by
T.J. (International) Ltd., Cornwall, PL28 8RW

CONTENTS

PROLOGUE

Just as the train was about to pull out from the station at Rome, a huge fat man came racing up the platform. He was accompanied by an equally elephantine woman and a swarm of children. With much shouting and gesticulating they pushed and shoved their way into my carriage and subsided laughing and breathless as the train gathered speed. The mother had barely recovered when she opened an enormous case and began doling out long loaves packed with greens and salami to each of her brood. There were eight children and even the baby was given a loaf. I was watching fascinated at the mountain of food disappearing when the father noticing, held out a loaf and offered it to me. I then became the cynosure of ten pairs of interested eyes, which brightened perceptibly when they realized I knew no Italian. They completely ignored my ignorance of their language and kept up a running stream of conversation, in unison, for the rest of my journey. As they were so obviously friendly, and full of good will, I felt it my duty to wear an expression of interest and smile when they gave me the cue. This enforced acting became rather a strain, and I was immensely relieved when we finally drew into a busy station, and I heard the cry 'Napoli, Napoli,' from the guard. All my train companions bade me an affectionate farewell, and I stepped out, dazed and slightly bewildered, at Naples Central Station.

A few months before, sitting amidst the last remnants of summer in Stephen's Green, Dublin, I had been stricken by a yearning for blue skies, warm seas, colourful people and above all, holding in my hand a bunch on which I had spent my last half-crown, above all – *freesias*. As I discussed this vision with my fellow nurses, the name of Mother Marie had come up. A byword in Irish households, she was the foundress of what had become an international order of nursing sisters. And so, as if by the intervention of some magic agency, here I was en route for her new hospital at Naples.

This huge Station surged with life and excitement. Demonstrative families kissed, wept and embraced as they welcomed or bade farewell to one another. Boys pushed hand-carts selling books, grapes and other fruit, or paper cartons of coffee. A football team were being seen off with the same adulation reserved in ancient times for gladiators.

Out of the crowd stepped a tall, thin,

elderly nun with a huge smile broadening as she approached. I have never felt more welcome in all my life. She told me her name was Sister Francis and she asked me questions about my journey as we bowled along in a taxi to the *Regina Maris*, as the hospital was called. The driver braked.

'There it is,' said Sister Francis, 'Do you like it?'

The hospital was a magnificent structure, five storeys high, and built on very contemporary lines. The whole building had an air of spaciousness and light, from the sweep of marble stairs in the huge all-glass hall to the flowing curves of the balconies which spanned every floor.

We climbed the marble staircase to the first landing.

'Our bedrooms are on your right and on the left is the Chapel and Sitting Room. There is also a room we used to keep for nuns on Retreat, that will be your bedroom, the bathroom is next door,' she explained as she shepherded me to my room.

Sister Francis (who was in charge of the hospital's catering and domestic affairs) then left to make some tea, and the other Sisters all popped in to welcome me. As well as Sister Francis and Sister Patrick, the Matron, there were Sister Margaret, Sister Jude, Sister Theresa, Sister Claire, Sister Joan, Sister Concepta, Sister Ann, Sister Bernadette and

Rev. Mother David, all of whom looked very alike to me that first night in their simple grey frocks and veils.

'I'm sure you are tired after your journey,' Sister Francis said kindly when she returned with the tea tray. 'We will leave you now to get some sleep. Don't get up until late tomorrow.' The Sisters bade me goodnight and left.

I went to bed a little apprehensive and a little excited by the step I had taken, but also immensely cheered by the sincere and warm welcome which had been given to me by the nuns.

CHAPTER 1

INITIATION

The following morning I awoke to the sound of soft chanting. My eyes flew open and for a moment I wondered where I was. I found myself in a narrow, oblong room rather like a shoe box. There was barely room for bed, dressing table, desk and chair. A few pictures had been added to give a homely touch, but nothing could detract from the fact that it was a nun's cell, even had the walls not been painted stark white, nor a crucifix hung over the door. I looked at my watch; it was 5 a.m. The chanting, I realized, came from the Chapel across the corridor, where the nuns were saying their morning prayers.

Bright sunshine poured into the room through my window and I could not resist hopping out of bed to peer out. A block of flats partially occluded my view of the bay, but this did not prevent my getting a glimpse of intense blue water, cloudless heavens and all the dazzling colour of the water-front, vivid in that bright sunshine. Even the flats across from me buzzed with life and activity at this early hour. Some of the women were beating carpets while others hustled about preparing breakfast. I was later informed that everyone arose early in Naples to finish their work before the noon heat. They had a short nap after dinner – the 'siesta' to balance their early rise.

During my first few days in Italy I led a lady's life. Meals were served in my room by a little Italian named Pia. She had half a dozen words of English which she proudly aired. 'You very welcome' was said with a broad smile. She was a very plain little creature, though exceptionally thoughtful and attentive.

It was fortunate that my meals were taken in private as my first encounter with spaghetti was not a particularly happy one. I either choked, or just missed the bite, or greater indignity, the long strings fell in yards from my chin like a horse eating hay. Eventually I learned how to make it sufficiently 'tacky' with a generous sprinkling of cheese, then to rotate my fork, until the unwieldy pieces were firmly wrapped around the prongs.

The hospital seamstress, a beautiful young girl, came and measured me for my new uniform. There was none of the battle usually necessary with hospital sewing women to prevent their putting one into a veritable bag. This young lady held the tape so tightly around my middle that I had to mime a plea to 'leave room for me to breathe'. Laughing, she released the tape a little and completed her measurements. Though neither of us spoke the other's language, she managed to introduce herself as Patrizia and tell me a little about herself. She was engaged to be married to someone *wonderful* and was kept very, very busy sewing her own trousseau after her work-day was completed. Her delightful spontaneous friendliness was my first introduction to the warm-hearted welcome accorded to strangers in Napoli, and when she left my room, I was convinced I should be happy among the Neapolitans.

The following day she had finished the uniform. It was a charming light blue dress with a white, peter pan collar and apron, and it fitted perfectly. Worn with white sandals I thought it looked cool and smart. Sister Margaret came in while I was trying it on. I was gradually getting to know the different faces. This face was young and gay and sported a pair of large, sparkling blue eyes. She was a trim little person and the rather shapeless habit she wore failed to conceal her neat figure and very shapely ankles.

This gay young Sister called out the door, 'Come in, Sister Concepta and see how nice Sheila looks in her new uniform.' Sister Concepta, a slight, ethereal little person, raised shy brown eyes and stammered her praise.

'I don't suppose it makes much difference *what* I look like if I can do my job all right,' I said with false modesty.

'Oh but it *does,*' they chorused, and Sister Concepta began to explain, quite seriously, how important it was in Naples to *'presenta bene'*, or have a presentable appearance. 'You could be the world's best nurse, but if you were too fat or ugly, you'd find it hard to get a job, and a beauty who was useless might get it before you.'

'It's the same in nearly every job in Naples,' Sister Margaret assured me.

'Look at Pia now (the maid who serves your meals). She is one of the best little workers we have in the hospital, but just because no one could call her a beauty, we had terrible trouble to take her to work. We don't own the *Regina Maris*. It belongs to a group of doctors and we only run it for them, so they have a definite word in the selection of staff. Sister Patrick solved the problem of Pia by 'slipping her in the back door' so to speak. She started work in our department and proved herself most reliable. She has been here six years now.'

'That was before our time,' interposed Sister Margaret, 'We have another year to go before we take our final vows.' There was a tap on the door and an older nun entered. This was Mother David, the Reverend Mother of the Convent, and the hospital pharmacist.

'Would you like me to show you around the hospital, Sheila?' she asked me. I was very anxious to see my new working conditions, so I accepted with alacrity.

We did a quick tour of the lovely building. All the front of the hospital was occupied by private rooms, each with its balcony and private bathroom, and all commanding a simply magnificent view of the Bay of Naples. Mother David pointed out to me, that in each room there was a long divan, which 'is turned into a bed at night for the company who is a relative or *parente*. No Italian patient will come into hospital without at *least* one relative and they sleep beside him too.' She laughed at my obvious amazement, 'Yes, we all found it strange in the beginning to have the family around when we are treating the patient, but one gets used to it and they are a help at times. We try to allow a maximum of two relatives per patient, but it is difficult to turn away Italian relatives as you'll see for yourself.' Sister Patrick then joined us and she said, 'We have two wards on each landing which are not supposed to have any company. Professor Caracciolo (the Chief Consultant of the hospital) goes mad if he sees too many relatives about the wards. By the way, I must introduce you to the Professor, here he is– '

Coming towards us was a short, fat, fair

man. He had the face of a well-fed baby and the gait of a penguin.

'What do I say to him?' I whispered.

'*Piacere* (pleased to meet you)' replied Sister Patrick.

She introduced us and I said '*Piacere*'. The Professor then spoke a few words to me in most appalling English, which I could not understand. I smiled vaguely and Sister Patrick replied gaily,

'Oh yes, Sir. She will indeed. Thank you very much.'

'What did he say?' I asked when the Professor, having patted my head and smiled benignly, passed on.

'Oh I haven't a notion,' Sister Patrick replied. 'He didn't know what I was saying either, but he likes to imagine he speaks English. He is very good to us,' she offered as a half-hearted excuse for her pleasant deception.

We continued our tour of inspection until each of the Sisters had shown me her department.

After lunch that afternoon, and in the next few days, the Sisters took me on walks in the vicinity of the hospital. What a colourful district it was too! A twisting road led up to a hill behind the hospital and from every corner one had breath-taking views of the colourful city and sea. Always too, there was the exquisite warmth of sunshine, penetrating, one felt, deep into the very blood. I had left bitter, biting cold behind to find this blessed warmth and 'liveness'.

I always enjoyed the walk down the Via Orazio but more especially on Sundays. The Sabbath was *the* day for weddings, and there was a constant procession of white-garbed brides to have the traditional wedding photograph taken overlooking the Bay. Most of the girls married young. Their traditional dress was a white crinoline, and, with their youthful seriousness, sharing the day with many other white-robed girls, they again looked like the little First Communicants of a few summers ago.

As I became better acquainted with the nuns, I discovered that I had been at school with two of the younger nuns, Sister Bernadette and Sister Margaret. They all did everything in their power to help me and make me feel at home. When I was out they left vases of beautiful flowers in my room, or perhaps a bar of Irish chocolate or some sweets. They often slipped in with welcome cups of tea, and even a hot-water bottle was delivered one evening when the Sisters, acclimatised to Italian heat, thought the day might seem cold to the newcomer.

The only Sister who seemed a little severe was the Matron, Sister Patrick. On my third day at the Clinic, she called at my room and in a rather clipped, precise voice, delivered herself of a long harangue, in which she warned me of the dangers in this fine city:—

'You can go out alone during the day, but don't talk to strangers, and just ignore these very annoying men who will insist on walking along beside you and eventually they will go away. It is most irritating the way they follow one, but they are quite harmless, I'm sure. It is at night that you must be careful. Never go out alone. The Italian girls at the *Regina Maris*, who live out, always have their fiancé, or a member of their family to meet them, if they are going home after eight.

'Now I'm no spoil-sport – no doubt you will have plenty of invitations from the men you meet, but there is one thing you should know here in Naples, and that is that there isn't the same free and easy friendship between the sexes which we know at home. A Neapolitan girl never goes out with a man, unless she is accompanied by a member of her family, until she becomes engaged to him. He is then called her *fidanzata*. Nearly all the girls have *fidanzati* and you will hear them talking about them.

'What I want to convey to you is that if you receive an invitation from a gentleman, please send him to me, and I will let you know whether you should accept or not.'

'All right Sister,' I replied. I understood perfectly what she was tactfully trying to convey, but I had difficulty in not smiling at the thought of Sister Patrick, of whom I was rather in awe, as my duenna. She skimmed rapidly to the next point in her lecture.

'As the bathroom next to your room is opposite the Chapel, I'm sure you will always be fully dressed going in and out. I had the greatest difficulty with the Italian nurses when they slept over here, as they were constantly running in and out in their underwear.' She closed the conversation by remarking kindly. 'If there is anything else you want to know, ask any of the Sisters.'

Later, Lucia, one of the Italian nurses took me into the Naples shopping centre. Though we could exchange no conversation, she linked her arm in mine and pointed to what she thought would interest me. The shops were exquisite and beautifully dressed. There were colourful open air cafes, many lovely fountains, and palm trees planted in groups about the City. In the central square dominated by an old Spanish Castle (relic of Spanish domination in Naples), the fountains were particularly fine. We stood for a while and watched the plumes of floodlit water rise and fall.

I thought Lucia an exceptionally nice girl. When I went on duty next day we were on the same ward and she was most helpful to the 'Irish Signorina'.

I started work on the third floor, which was

for acute surgery and brain operations. Sister Bernadette, who was in charge of the floor, gave me a brief tour of inspection, also a list of the Italian names for many of the articles used in nursing. She rapidly dictated the Italian for medicines and dressings, trolleys and thermometers, injections and syringes, masks and stethoscopes, until I began to wonder how I had ever mastered all the tools of my trade, even in English. Sister next introduced me to all the people with whom I would work. Sister Bernadette explained,

'On this landing we have three trained nurses, or "diploma" nurses, as they are called, as well as yourself.'

I was very pleased to see that Lucia was also on my ward, as I felt that this slim, dark girl and I could be friends, though I did not even speak her language. We did become firm friends later, and her good humour and spontaneous wit were always a delight. On my first morning she took over the introductions when Sister Bernadette was called away. She indicated the other two 'diplomas', Carla and Gina – Carla, huge, fat and jolly looking, Gina, beautiful but sulky. When I knew Gina better, I found her beauty very superficial, for she was bad tempered and childishly spiteful.

Carla came from the North of Italy. Generally speaking the Northern Italians were more efficient than their Southern sisters, and, as I later discovered, Carla was no exception. She was inclined to look down her nose at the Southerners. 'All they are good for is singing and sun-bathing, and they think that they have a monopoly on love-making,' she would sniff.

Every Neapolitan will argue that Vesuvius makes his blood hot and really believes it himself. 'I have no patience with the lazy South,' Carla declared, 'No wonder all the industry and riches are in the North where people know how to work.' She was a bit too outspoken in her criticism, and the Southerners did not take it all lying down.

'Bah, you had to come down here to warm your toes. Why, in Milano we are told that they have to heat the pavements in winter. Here we are in the land of eternal sunshine. Have you sun like this in your Milanese winter? Have you a bay as blue? Blossoms all the year round? Singers and song writers like Naples? Or anything to touch our Neapolitan cookery?'

'*Uh fa,*' Carla spat, 'No one in Naples can cook, ah,' she sighed, 'the Milanese cooking is world famous. Why the food here is only good for making one fat!' This was a statement confirmed in the flesh. Everyone laughed and the arguments were momentarily discontinued, to be resumed on the least provocation. Though Carla was critical of her compatriots, they were quick to appreciate her Northern efficiency, which they admired, but never hoped to achieve. I noticed that there was a tremendous difference between the nurses and people from different regions of the country. The further North one travelled, the more calm the people appeared in temperament, while the further south one went the more Latin the temperament, until, below Rome, one met the typical happy-go-lucky, singing, laughing, hot-blooded, hot-tempered, love-making Italian of popular imagination.

On this, my first morning, all their characters were unknown to me, and all I saw was three smiling faces trying to surmount the barrier of language.

They were all very friendly and anxious to make me feel at home. Finally someone offered to make me a cup of tea, and I was hustled off to the kitchen. Behind the door, two other nurses were having a quick cup of coffee; they laughed and put one finger to their lips.

'Just like Dublin,' I thought, when a nurse who had missed breakfast would have a delicious, forbidden cup of tea behind the kitchen door. In the meantime, Antonetta, a *ragazza*, as the maids were called, was making my tea. She had water boiling in a pot on the gas, to which she added a little paper bag of tea leaves, then sugar and a piece of lemon, stirring gaily all the time.

'*E buona?* – is good?' she demanded, as she handed me a cup of this solution. I can take lemon juice, so I nodded vigorously that her tea was divine. This had the effect of making Antonetta a keen tea-maker and she was constantly calling me for a cup of the brew, while the others stood around, and I enviously watched them guzzling delicious cups of steaming coffee.

(I was some time in the hospital before I hit on a plan to dispense with the tea and obtain some of that divine coffee. Entering the kitchen I announced to Antonetta 'from now on I wish to be 'proprio Italiana' – real Italian. I will speak Italian, sing Italian, wear Italian clothes, eat Italian food and drink Italian coffee,' I finished slyly. This announcement was received with wild approval. Having kissed me soundly, Antonetta called in the rest of the staff. After quite an orgy of kisses and embraces, I got what I had planned, when Antonetta poured out large cups of coffee for all, including her new 'convert'.)

CHAPTER 2

GETTING TO KNOW YOU

In the dining room we were waited upon by two young ragazzas and my old acquaintance Pia, who, I noted, was very much the boss. She shouted and ordered about the other two maids, who paid very little attention to her row, but continued serving with complete indifference. Pia was extremely efficient and took pride in her excellent service.

'When Pia is on duty the menus are never mixed,' she would say, with a scowl at her two guilty assistants, or, 'When Pia is on duty the Signorinas never have to wait to be served'. It was perfectly true, although she was extremely noisy and inclined to shout too much, to sing at the top of her voice and even to break the china when in a temper: she was also the most reliable person in the domestic staff. Nurses, too late to sign their menu, could leave it to Pia, and she knew the likes and dislikes of each girl so well that each would receive eminently suitable fare. If one of the Signorinas was not eating well it was a personal affair of hers. She would take away the untouched dish and return with some little speciality and an injunction, 'Try this, it is very light and tasty' – *'deve mangiare bene'* – 'you must eat well' was her stock phrase.

The food at the *Regina Maris* was very good indeed. Every morning the nurses were presented with the Menu Card from which they chose whatever they wished to eat during the day. The girls sat over their breakfast, (the typical Continental-style meal of rolls and coffee) and earnestly discussed what they would eat today. Many of them were faddy about their meals, so the hospital had found it easier to allow them to choose their own diets, then listen to the complaints if they did not like the meals served.

This method also appealed to the girls, as they could go on slimming diets, vegetable diets or whatever the fashion decreed. Certainly the food was healthy – huge slices of cheese, every kind of vegetable and fruit, was served in abundance, bunches of grapes, apricots, peaches, and enormous oranges were a treat to enjoy. At first the Sisters filled in my menu for the day, but after a few weeks, it was considered I should enjoy my meals more if I chose them myself. They surmised that I now knew the names of the dishes, but in fact I did not. I had lazily allowed the nuns to fill my stomach without bothering to know what I was eating. The first morning I had to do my own menu I read through the list, but as none of it made sense, I decided to ask one of the cooks to write for me. He had spoken a few words of broken English to me earlier in the week. Ugo would do so with pleasure. At dinner he came into the dining room – 'You like? Eat well?' 'Yes thank you.'

At supper the same performance occurred.

The following day at dinner, he informed me that he had a nice little scooter, wouldn't I like to take a trip? I decided I had better write my own menu.

My pride would not allow me to admit my ignorance, therefore I decided I would write three articles from the list each day, keep a record of what appeared and in a short time I would know all the dishes. Unfortunately, to gain experience one must suffer! My suffering took the form of most peculiar meals for some time. I would come down to lunch feeling ravenous, to find two plates of clear soup and two apples. Not quite my idea of lunch, but when the other Signorinas asked 'not hungry Sheila?' I would stubbornly shake my head. Conversely, they must have been surprised the day I ordered three plates of different types of heavy *pasta*. Eventually I mastered the art of menu-planning, and later when Cathleen, another Irish girl, arrived, I was able to help her.

As I found it so difficult to order my own

meals, it was fortunate that we never had to trouble about the patients' diets. Every morning a very spruce young man appeared at Sister Bernadette's desk. In ten minutes he ran through the list of patients. The only information he required from Sister was the list of new patients or operation cases and special diets. 'One, four and eleven are normal diets but fasting after dinner, the new patient in 14 is a diabetic on two thousand calories, No. 28 is fat free, No. 30 high protein and No. 32 low residue.' Salvatore, briefed on the special diets, bowed and departed to do his round of every room where, with infinite patience and tact, he would help the relatives choose from the menu a diet suitable to the patient's requirements. By artistic descriptions of the food he would tempt unwilling appetites. He was also a blessing in disguise when anorexic patients complained bitterly to us that the food was inedible. 'I will speak to Salvatore for you,' we would say, thus shifting responsibility for one complaint. Salvatore would arrive the following morning with his usual tact: he never argued that the food was always perfect and the catering staff first class. Instead, 'Tell me what you really enjoy,' he would tell the grumbler, 'and I personally will see that you get the choice servings.'

The meals continued as before with no

extra effort on Salvatore's part and it was no more than his due when the patient on leaving, pressed a note into his hand in grateful appreciation of his personal attention.

These first few weeks in the hospital were a time of great mental stimulation for me. I was learning a new language, studying new nursing techniques and getting to know so many strangers. I was also getting rid of many of my preconceived opinions.

I had always been led to believe that Italians were an extremely impatient race. Though true, this certainly did not apply to the medical staff. They would wait patiently for ages for a nurse to assist them. On one occasion, the Orthopaedic Specialist, Professor Morelli, asked me for a pair of plaster shears to remove the plaster from a patient in the treatment room.

'I'll have to go to the Theatre for them,' I replied, and left him.

When I reached the Theatre, Sister Margaret grabbed my arm, 'Here, Sheila, watch this patient a moment, will you?' and she rushed off, leaving me to support the jaw of an unconscious patient. Ten minutes later a nurse relieved me and Sister Margaret turned to me. 'Sorry to press you into service, but that "gom" booked the Theatre last night for ten today and when I asked him, 'Which operation?' he replied, "Oh, only a bit of nonsense". Well, his bit of nonsense turned out to be a bone graft! You can imagine, we had nothing ready. All the morning's work has been thrown out and there is a Caesar booked for two this afternoon. After that emergency last night I won't have enough dressings if we don't autoclave some now.' She was busy packing dressings into a drum as she spoke.

'Sister, can you come here a moment?' the Ophthalmic Surgeon called from the scrubbing-up room. His mask was slipping and he wished Sister to tighten the strings, otherwise he would have to re-commence scrubbing.

Forgetting my original quest, I packed Sister Margaret three drums and put them in the autoclave and returned to my ward. Absent-mindedly I sauntered into the treatment room. Morelli turned to me, 'Have you the shears, nurse?' he asked, quite pleasantly. I bolted and returned in a few seconds. 'Here they are, Sir.'

'Good girl, just support this leg now.'

Not a word of rebuke for making him wait a half-hour!

Hardly had I cleared the treatment room of plaster-of-Paris when Lorenzotti, an eminent brain surgeon, and Signorina Carla entered with a patient.

'We are going to take a sample of your blood,' the Professor explained to his patient, as Signorina Carla tightened the tourniquet on his arm.

'Where are you from, Signore Tosti?' asked the Professor of his patient, as he slipped the needle into the vein.

'Sorrento,' the man replied.

'Ah, Sorrento,' sighed Lorenzotti, and broke into the opening bars of the famous melody 'Torna Sorrento'. As he drew off the blood into his syringe, the patient and nurse Carla joined in the air. With obvious enjoyment, the trio finished their song.

I found the patients very temperamental. They would fly into a furious rage and two minutes later be all smiles. One minute they were threatening to tell the Matron that they had had to wait two minutes for their injection and the next they were kissing my hand and saying it was the 'Madonna Herself' who sent me to Italy.

Every room had its crowd of interfering, annoying, inquisitive and rarely helpful relatives, known as *parente*. When a new patient arrived and had not yet undressed, I often found it difficult to decide which one of the milling crowd was the sick one. Finally I developed a technique to overcome this difficulty. I would enter the room, stopping at the threshold as I had been taught and ask, 'Con permesso?' – 'May I come in?' Patient and relatives replied in chorus 'prego avanti' – 'please enter'. Then I would explain, 'I have to make an injection,' meanwhile

32

preparing my syringe.

The relatives asked, 'What is it?' – 'What is it for?' – 'Who ordered it?'

All questions having been answered politely, one of the crowd either hoisted a skirt or lowered pants, and I knew my victim. The patient begged, 'Gently, gently if you please.' I replied, 'This will not hurt, it will make you better. *Ecco*, it is done. How brave you are!' The patient yelled and wept. The relatives wept and rushed to hold his hand or smooth his brow. I looked heart-broken. If only I could have managed a tear at this point I should have been accepted forever! The patient smiled tremulously and I said, 'You are so courageous.' He replied, 'You are so good, kind and gentle.' With exchanges of flattery and compliments I asked permission – and left.

I regretfully realised that the unquest-ioning faith in their nurses, bestowed by the patients at home, was not to be a feature of Italy. Every procedure required a lengthy explanation before the Italian was satisfied that he should accept treatment. They all knew far more than the average layman about their anatomy, ailments and treat-ment. I found too that they had very fixed ideas which were impossible to alter. Venti-lation for instance, was often a bone of con-tention. On a sweltering morning we could enter a room where three or four people, including the patient, had spent the night. The place would be sealed tight. The first thing I always did was to open a window, which would be promptly closed the minute I turned my back. The people were terrified of draughts. The relatives also caused quite unnecessary discomfort to our patients by making them wear far too many clothes. On a day when we were suffering with the heat, it was not unusual to enter a room and find one's patient dripping with perspiration, and wrapped like a cocoon in various layers of woollen vests, pyjamas, jacket and complete with scarf, bed-socks and night cap.

The idea of 'suffering in silence' was another plan of which they did not approve. For the smallest pain they opened their mouths and bellowed. At first this unrestrained abandon to pain caused me great concern.

When a strong young man held his belly and roared and even wept with dolour, I naturally considered he was an extremely urgent case, and called immediately for the Doctor, meanwhile staying by his bedside to give him comfort and allay his fears. He lapped up the sympathy and comfort until the Doctor came and pronounced a mild case of cramp. I was not entirely convinced that the pain had been mild until I heard the same fellow fifteen minutes later reading the riot act that his portion of spaghetti was too small.

Most of the nursing techniques were the same as I had been used to at home, but there were also many differences. The patients had great faith in injections and many drugs which would have been given orally at home were given by injection. This meant that the poor patients were constantly being stuck with needles. They seemed to feel however, that *something* was being done for them if they had injections, and many were quite indignant if they were not having them.

It was also strange to me that the thermometers were on the Centigrade instead of Fahrenheit scale and were big and awkward compared with the narrow tubes used at home. These thermometers were left under the arm for a full five minutes, and woe betide the nurse who tried to remove it sooner. The patient and his relatives conscientiously timed the 'cooking' to the last second!

They also had a morbid fear of catching cold.

One old lady visited her husband, an hotel owner, who was having a cataract extraction. She was so precise about not catching cold that she left the husband's room on the fifth floor wearing her dress; on the fourth floor she stopped the lift, got out and added a jumper; on the third floor, a cardigan, and so on. Items of apparel were added until she reached the 'even temperature' of street level, where she would emerge bundled up like a teddy-bear.

A peculiarity of Neapolitan medicine was that although they used the very latest methods and equipment, some very old-fashioned treatments were still employed. The application of bags of ice was a particularly awkward type of treatment ordered when there was a danger of internal haemorrhage. We believed that these cold, lumpy objects placed on the abdomen caused far more discomfort and loss of sleep than their doubtful worth justified, but the doctors believed they helped to prevent bleeding. In the battle of wills the doctors won and we were constantly employed breaking ice and re-filling ice bags which quickly melted in the heat and had to be re-filled. How I hated to see the order for 'continuous ice bags' on the report sheets.

Still worse was the treatment of congestion by the application of leeches. Those loathsome blood-sucking creatures filled me with revulsion.

The Ophthalmic Surgeon was the worst offender where the use of leeches was concerned. It was while taking his report on one of his sailor patients I received my first order to apply a leech.

'Keep him on the Diamox tablets, continue Eserine drops hourly and apply four

36

leeches.' He indicated the outer canthus of the eye and behind the ear where the leeches were to bite. The theory was that the leeches, with their sharp little teeth, would make an incision in the flesh and suck out sufficient blood to relieve congestion and pain. Not only did they draw off the blood themselves, but they secreted a substance into the wound which prevented its clotting, thus causing further bleeding. 'Altogether a horrible idea,' I shuddered as I entered the ward, carrying the cotton wool, bandages, salt, scentless soap and water and the awful bowl of leeches. My patient, the old sailor, was very co-operative. When I explained the procedure to him he answered, 'I don't mind, Signorina, I've had them before, on my chest, for pneumonia. I would stand anything to relieve this pain in my eye.'

The other five occupants of the ward watched with interest as I placed the cape around my patient's shoulders and proceeded to wash the areas to be bitten, with the unscented soap, as leeches apparently do not like perfume. Next, I gingerly picked up the soft, slimy little animal with a piece of cotton wool and put his head to the patient's skin. In theory he should have bitten the area: in practice the horrid little beastie had no intention of biting the dried-up, weather-beaten, leathery skin of the intended victim. He would prefer the soft, white flesh of the inside of my wrist, and swung his mouth towards this point. Forgetting all dignity and decorum, with a yelp, I dropped cotton wool, leeches and all on the floor and retreated a safe distance. I was quite shaking with terror at the thought of these blood-sucking things attached to my flesh. My reaction caused peals of merriment in the ward. They were kind-hearted though, and their amusement was quickly followed by compassion. Another young sailor slipped out of bed and offered to do the job for me. He was absolutely fearless and even picked the leeches up in his hands. 'They won't bite me, they only like sweet folk,' he twinkled. I was then dispatched to the kitchen for sugared milk, drops of which my helper placed on the strategic points of the old man's face. The sailor spoke encouragingly to the leech as he applied it – 'Come, come, eat, eat. It's good. *Mangia, mangia, brava, da brava,*' as the leech took hold. The animals bit and attacked by their mouths and held on to the skin, sucking. I stood grimly by the bedside clutching the salt which, when applied to their heads, would make them release their grip. 'It is all right Signorina, you can leave if you like and I'll look after them,' my helper offered kindly.

'No think you, I'll stay,' I replied, fearing the leech would release his hold and maybe

38

injure the patient's eye if I did not watch them.

In horrified fascination I watched the revolting bodies undulating in their ghastly task. My eyes dilating in fear, I saw their bodies grow fat. Sweat broke out on my forehead and my vision blurred. In a dizzy blur I saw my helper shake salt on the animals and remove them and then place a pad of cotton wool on the old man's face.

The mist cleared and I found myself surrounded by five concerned sailors in pyjamas, one patting my hand, another smoothing my brow, while my former helper pressed a glass into my hand. 'Here, drink this.' I drank the wine and immediately felt ashamed of my loss of dignity. I apologised to the men, especially the old man whom I felt had undergone a worse ordeal than I.

'It is nothing, Signorina,' he replied, 'I understand perfectly that the bravest women are afraid of little animals. It is just their make-up I suppose' – he laughed, 'Anyway, your treatment has done me great good. I have no pain now.'

Besides getting to know my patients, the nursing and medical staff, the nurses also introduced me to friends outside the hospital.

I was but a fortnight at the hospital when Lucia – (Sister acting as interpreter) – asked me would I care to visit the circus with herself and her fiancé. I was delighted, in spite of the fact that neither spoke the other's language, we set out quite merrily.

Lucia's fiancé Johnny, was waiting in his car outside the hospital, and he went out of his way to be attentive to Lucia and her friend. Though they spoke no English and I spoke no Italian, we still managed to converse with the aid of mime and my pocket dictionary.

The evening was a great success and before I left them we had planned to make a foursome with one of Johnny's friends for a night at the opera.

When I returned to my room from the Circus, Sister Joan (who shared with Sister Margaret the responsibilities of the operating theatre) brought me a cup of tea and some sandwiches.

'Was it any good?' she asked.

'Super,' I replied enthusiastically. 'It was the same circus which performed at Christmas for His Holiness,' I continued, 'and I was allowed to hold the lion cub which was presented to The Pope in my arms! It was a *splendid* show with not a break in the performance from beginning to end. Their men were terribly handsome and the girls exquisite. You never saw anything as breathtaking as the acrobatics. Oh, but Sister, you should have seen the lion-tamer! – absolutely fearless. He even put his head in the lion's mouth. He was dressed in white tropical uniform and was madly handsome.'

'I'm afraid you have fallen for the lion-tamer, but it's no use my dear,' Sister Joan smiled, 'he is already married.'

'How do you know?'

'He was in here as a patient and was shaking with terror before his operation! After it he was one of the best patients we ever nursed. When he went home his wife invited us to tea in his wagon. It was a beautiful home-on-wheels and we had a lovely tea.'

She left me with a new respect for these little nuns, who thought nothing of taking afternoon tea with the handsomest man I had ever seen, and a lion-tamer to boot!

My evening at the circus encouraged me to think that I could manage very well in Italy without the language. I felt otherwise though, when I realized that I had some shopping to do. My requirements were simple and few. At home a fifteen-minute trip to the nearest shop would have sufficed. Here I was faced with apparently insurmountable problems. My small list would first have to be translated. Then I would need to take a tram to the shopping centre. 'Which tram? Which stop? Where would I get off? How does one ask for a ticket? How would I know how much money to pay?' These and other questions were revolving in my head when I discovered that the Sisters, always considerate, had solved them.

41

'Would you like to go shopping? I'll take you,' Sister Bernadette offered.

Had I realized quite how formidable an undertaking was the tram ride alone, I'm sure I should never have considered venturing on my own. When the already packed tram stopped in front of us and the folding door slid open, I was swept in a sudden wild stampede into the crowded interior. The folding door slammed shut, almost amputating the legs and decapitating the heads of those attempting to follow me. Wedged tightly between bodies there was barely room to expand one's lungs to breathe.

The conductor on his little stool, protected from the squash by an encircling iron rail, shouted and gesticulated madly. *'Avanti, avanti'* – 'onward, onward'. Was he joking? I wondered. Where did he expect them to go? The passengers were pushing onward, onward, leaving me less and less breathing space.

'Come on, Sheila,' called Sister Bernadette. 'We will have to make our way to the top, or else we'll never be able to get off at our stop.'

Aided by elbows and shoves, the polite 'excuse me' and *permesso*, we fought through the impenetrable walls of humanity until, reaching the upper door of the 'bus, we were disgorged breathless, and dishevelled at our stop.

'One can only enter the 'bus by the rear door and must exit by the top one – by the driver,' Bernadette explained. She was quite unruffled by the crush of our 'bus ride. With brisk efficiency she strode through the shops, her grey veil flying and a purposeful frown on her forehead. The shopping was done in record time. We were soon seated again in the packed 'bus for our return journey. I was awed and impressed by Sister Bernadette's efficiency and economy of time – not a moment had been wasted.

When we got off our 'bus, we began to hurry towards the hospital when Sister suddenly stopped short, her head on one side and a delightful smile on her face. 'A barrel organ,' she beamed. Then I too heard the gay, tinkling music. The organ grinder was a short distance along the street, busily grinding out the merry notes. Our hurry forgotten, Sister Bernadette and I followed the music-maker as he pushed his organ to the next block of flats. After each performance he received a shower of ten lira pieces from the women in the flats above his head. Between each tune Sister Bernadette would sigh, then 'We'll listen to just *one* more' and we would follow on to the next stop. Suddenly, in the middle of a lively rendering of 'Funiculi funicula', Sister suddenly glanced at her watch and gave a yelp, 'Madonna mia. I'll be late for prayers' and

43

we practically ran all the way back to the hospital.

This pleasant outing awoke my ambition to speak Italian. I could not forever be tied to the nun's apron strings, and besides, I reminded myself, I owed a duty to my patients – to understand them. Not only had I the difficulty of understanding the Italians, but the Sisters had developed a language of their own (which I was later to adopt) of speaking a mixture – half English, half Italian. As they were quite unaware of this peculiarity, they must have found me excessively stupid at times in those first weeks. Those first weeks on duty – shall I ever forget them? My brain whirled with the series of new impressions, new people and new methods, while my tongue tied itself in knots as I tried to express myself.

I received much sympathy and consolation from the Sisters about the difficulty of learning Italian. I lapped up this sympathy, but to my shame did very little hard study. In fact I took things rather easy. When I was invited to watch the exciting car races I accepted gratefully. A visit to the Napoli Zoo I accepted also. When the following day I was invited to visit a famous 'Ristorante', I did not hesitate to say yes. The day after my visit to the Ristorante, Sister Patrick met me on the corridor. She fixed me with a stern eye and demanded.

'How did you spend your off-duty yesterday?'

'At the "Ristorante"'.

'And the day before?'

'At the Zoo'.

'And the day before?'

'The car races,' I faltered.

'And the day before?' she continued inexorably.

'The Circus,' I replied, beginning to feel guilty.

'*And when*, my dear girl, did you find time to study, in the past four days?'

I had to admit I hadn't opened a book.

Then ensued the most severe 'dressing-down' I had ever received. I saw how lazy, idle and selfish I had been and felt ashamed.

My shame took refuge in anger. 'I'll show her,' I vowed. 'I'll speak this language if it kills me.'

Had I but known it at the time, this was exactly the effect the wise Sister Patrick had wished to achieve.

Without the aid of a teacher or the stimulus of another pupil, my progress was slow.

We had at this time in the hospital, a young woman dying of a brain tumor. Night and day her mother watched by the bedside, spoon-feeding her meals with infinite patience, and ready to call the nurses if she noticed her daughter required attention. In cases like this one, where the patient would always need someone in attendance, it was a splendid help to the staff to have a relative at hand. The Signora Corri was an exceptionally intelligent woman and therefore doubly welcome. I felt sorry for her in her lonely task and we would chat together in English as I attended her daughter. She told me she was a professor of languages and one day asked me, 'Who is teaching you Italian?' I explained, 'I teach myself and the Sisters help me when they are free.'

'Why not come to me in your off-duty and I will give you lessons?'

Thus began a very strict tutorship. The Signora Corri was a stern teacher and never liked to correct a mistake twice. 'There you go again Miss Sheila,' she would chide in her very correct English, 'the same mistake again.'

'Repeat this exercise tomorrow and rule an adequate margin.'

I was back at school again, but grateful for the expert teaching I received. It was gratifying also to see the Signora forget her sorrows in the concentration required in teaching. Occasionally she even surprised herself by laughing heartily at my comic mistakes.

'I will give you the verb *uscire*, to decline, for tomorrow, then we will have more laughter,' she would smile. 'If there is any useful sentences you wish to translate, tell me and we will do it together,' she told me once. From that day forward I had a list of words and sentences to be translated as, 'This will not hurt!'

'I'm sorry I have a previous engagement,' she twinkled at this and laughed heartily when I asked her to translate.

'Please do not shout. It does not help me to understand better.'

Many foreigners feel that if one does not understand their language, it follows that one is deaf. Amata, a small Neapolitan assistant nurse was a notorious sinner in this respect. When I did not understand at once, she would practically blast my ear drums with a roar. This invariably had the effect of making me lose my head and be unable to understand the simplest word. The next time Amata employed her shouting tactics, she was stunned when in faultless Italian, I trotted out my neat sentence.

'Sorry Sheila,' she faltered. Then being an intelligent and warm-hearted little creature, she soon learned the simple way to make me understand, to twist a sentence another way perhaps, to speak clearly and above all slowly, and of course, she made adequate use of gestures. It was astonishing to see how much an Italian could convey by facial expression or gesture alone. The mere crook of a finger or raising of an eyebrow could convey a wealth of meaning. These gestures

47

were so useful and so explanatory that it was not long before I found myself using them. I noticed the Sisters also did a great deal of talking with their hands and when I asked Sister Bernadette how a certain patient was faring and she extended her hand with a see-saw movement, I knew he was 'cosi-cosi' or 'fair to middling'. This capacity to talk without words was practically demonstrated by patients who had throat operations.

One particular case I remember, a great big farmer who had a laryngectomy (removal of the 'voice-box') for cancer, positively amazed me. He scorned the writing tablet and pencil, always provided for these patients, and would carry on long conversations with his relatives by using his hands.

'What did he say?' I would ask his daughter.

'He wants to know when you will stop feeding him by tube' or 'When can I eat spaghetti?'

And when she translated a long, flattering speech of extravagant superlatives, I was ready to doubt that a few facial and hand movements could convey so much, until she translated gesture by gesture what had been 'said'.

We had an added language difficulty in the fact that in Italy every region has its own dialect. This can differ so much from the pure Italian as to be almost another language. We often had patients from the country whom even the Italian nurses could not understand. The nursing of these cases was often a matter of instinct. We had to imagine the symptoms the patient suffered and, relying on training and imagination, visualize what he needed. Sometimes we had quite a performance bringing various things to the bedside until finally, arriving with maybe a bottle of Sangemini water, one knew at once it was the correct thing by the smiles and nods of approval.

There was one very pleasant woman in No. 14 whose dialect I found particularly difficult. However, by speaking slowly I always managed to understand what she wanted. I had to admire the way her face would suffuse with pleasure when I understood and obtained what she required, in spite of my insufferable slowness.

One day I went into the treatment room, where the staff were preparing treatment trays.

'Listen girls,' I said, 'I'd prefer it if one of you answered 14's bell. I find her dialect very difficult and she is such a charming person, I hate trying her patience.'

'But Sheila, we were letting you answer her bell deliberately. We don't understand Spanish!'

'Spanish?' I asked incredulous. Seeing my

astonishment, they all laughed heartily.

What I had thought was a dialect was actually another language!

I felt rather stupid and a little embarrassed when answering Villa's bell. When the buzzer rang and I noticed the light over his room, I quickly found myself another job in the hope that one of my colleagues would answer it. I found them very reluctant to do so. One day when I had brought him his medicine, he caught my arm, 'Sheila, give me a kiss?' I delivered a stinging slap on the detaining hand and swept from the room, seething with indignation. The next time his bell rang I made no attempt to answer it – neither did anyone else. Lucia asked coaxingly, 'Answer him, will you, Sheila?'

'I will not,' I replied vehemently. They looked at me curiously, 'Has he been annoying you, too?' It turned out that the old *Roué* had made unwelcome advances to every member of the staff.

'No wonder his fracture won't set. Rosario knocked him on the floor when he tried to embrace her,' Amata told me.

Sister Concepta (who was relieving on our floor) interrupted our discussion.

'No. 2 has been ringing for the past ten minutes and no one has answered his bell.'

We looked at one another. Not one of us felt like explaining to the childlike little nun the reason for our reluctance to answer the bell. Finally I said, 'Come on Rosario, we'll both answer it,' thereby setting a precedent of behaviour. From then on we always answered his bell in twos. This infuriated the old fellow but he had no grounds for complaint. 'I rang for one nurse,' he groused. 'And you have two' we answered sweetly. The difficulty about always answering in pairs meant that sometimes Villa's bell was left some time unanswered while we scouted around for a second nurse. He complained bitterly to Sister Concepta, who, not understanding our reasons, spoke reprovingly to us. Finally he complained to Sister Patrick who descended on us like an avenging angel.

'Why isn't Villa's bell being answered?' We all looked sheepish. Suddenly with a flash of intuition she asked, 'He hasn't been unpleasant, has he?'

With a rush of confidence everyone launched her complaints.

Without further comment Sister Patrick left us and repaired to Room 2.

When she emerged some twenty minutes later she called the staff.

'You will have no further trouble from Signore Villa. I want you to answer his bell immediately in future so that he will have no further cause for complaint. You can now return to your duties.'

Though I had no further trouble with Signore Villa, there were still other crosses to bear in mastering the Italian 'lingua'. The Director of the hospital, Professor Caracciolo, had a great joke which he would enact for the benefit of his three assistants. 'Do you speak Italian now?' He would ask and chuck me under the chin, and then laugh heartily as if the idea that I should ever speak the language was preposterous. Though this game annoyed me intensely and I could, if I had tried, have strung one or two words together to show I was not entirely speechless, yet when he asked the favourite question I was usually overcome by shyness at the four pairs of amused eyes and I remained mute. Then as the Professor departed on his rounds Treves, one of the housemen who was forever laughing at my Italian, would look back at me and bite his lip in imitation of my habit, leaving me in an impotent fury.

'I'll show them,' I vowed for the second time. When I went to my lesson one afternoon I handed my teacher a large sheet of closely packed writing.

'What is this?' she asked in surprise, 'a speech?'

'Yes, Signorina, it is a speech which I want you to help me translate into Italian. I want to have plenty to say to the Professor,' and I explained about my mortification each morning. She *did* laugh.

'Very well, I agree. It will improve your vocabulary and the Professor will get a surprise.'

That evening, from time to time, I would remove a little piece of paper from my pocket and mumble my 'speech'–

'No, I do not speak the language very well, yet, Professor, but I am learning. Every day I add some new words to my vocabulary and I believe my grammar has improved. Certainly my pronunciation cannot be described as perfect, but I am trying hard to improve that defect.' The speech continued on these lines, making me as loquacious as I had formerly been mute.

The other Signorinas shared in the joke and they would 'hear' my speech to make sure I was word perfect. Amata heard the speech so often that when a patient asked me 'How are you getting on with the language?' and I trotted out my speech in reply, she was able to prompt me when I broke down.

Unfortunately the Professor tired of his game and I never had a chance to air my prose. The effort was well rewarded when my former tormentor Treves, entered a patient's room and I said 'Buena Sera – good evening, doctor'.

'Oh! – good evening, Signorina, so you now speak Italian!' he jeered.

53

I could have hugged myself with delight at the amazed incredulity of his expression as in a light conversational tone I ran on and on with my monologue.

'It is miraculous,' I heard him gasp, as I made a quick exit before he got his breath back to question me on my fantastic new grasp of the language.

CHAPTER 3

NEAPOLITANS AND NUNS

The Italians' behaviour in chapel appeared most unusual to me, accustomed as I was to our rather frigid ways. They would greet each other, even shake hands and thought nothing of a little chat. In most of the churches there were no benches: one hired a chair instead for 10 lire. A woman would pick up her chair and deposit it beside a neighbour for a chat. Then they would spot another friend across the aisle and give a sibilant hiss – *p-s-s-s* – to attract her attention, 'And how is your liver?' one asked the other kindly. Between gossip they would blow a few kisses to the Madonna, The Sacred Heart and the popular San Antonio. They were always surrounded by children of all ages, who crawled though the chairs, pulled each other's hair or kissed one another with Latin abandon. The mothers went to Communion accompanied by toddlers or carrying babies in their arms. The children chattered incessantly. The mother might turn to her child and say 'Blow a kiss to baby Jesu', and the little one obliged very gracefully. The people behaved in Church almost the same as they did in their own home. I even saw a woman breast-feed her baby in the chapel.

I must admit that some of the Catholic ceremonies held in Italy were marathon. The ceremonies in honour of The Madonna of Pompeii went on for three days in which the people invoked our Lady under the title of Queen of The Rosary, for their requests. They came to the magnificent Basilica in their thousands, whole families carrying cases of food to sustain them for their days of prayer. In between rosaries and invocations they sat on the Church steps and partook of huge loaves filled with spinach or salami or hard-boiled eggs. Bottles of coffee were passed around afterwards. The people stayed up all one night praying, the children curled up asleep on the benches, in their parents' arms or at the foot of one of the side altars, wrapped in an overcoat and creating a very angelic picture of childhood innocence.

Pompeii Basilica was also a popular Church for First Communicants. The little girls, very conscious of themselves and of their important event, were always dressed exquisitely in long white dresses. Like child brides, they knelt around the altar, the epitome of untouched grace and beauty.

Their religion was a very real part of their

lives – the Madonna and Child considered as part of the family, hence no doubt, the strange familiarity with God and His Saints.

One morning I was awakened by a terrible row outside my bedroom door. I heard the Lord's Name over and over again. Feeling sure a battle royal was on outside my door, I took a peep. I beheld Signora B., whose husband had been admitted the previous evening with a serious head injury. Now the Signora was praying at the pitch of her lungs to the Statue of The Sacred Heart, which stood in the corridor outside my door.

'My Peppino was always so devout and so good to his relatives,' she bellowed. 'He was always giving you and the Saints presents. Remember the lovely silver heart he sent you and it cost 2,000 lire? I've got faith in you.' Now and then she would give the statue a pat on the cheek which was almost a wallop.

Three Sisters, Ann, Bernadette and Concepta came out of the Chapel to try to quieten the woman a little before the Mass. It was impossible either to quieten her or disentangle her arms, which were now entwined firmly around the statue. As the image was rocking perilously on its pedestal and the Parroco (our Parish Priest) was due for Mass in a few minutes, I wondered what the Sisters would do. They rose to the occasion as always. Sister Ann and Bernadette lifted down the statue, while Concepta called the lift and escorted the Signora, together with her statue, to her husband's room. The woman was beaming and all the relatives very pleased when the huge statue was set up at the foot of Peppi's bed, there to remain until he left the hospital, hale and hearty. We knew that his first call on the way home was to the little Church of Maria del Parto to donate another silver heart to his Lord.

When I recounted this event to Sister Margaret, one day when Sister Patrick found her using rubber tubing as a skipping rope, she announced, 'I think I would give a little silver heart myself if I could only improve. How I wish I could be like Sister Concepta, although,' she chuckled, 'her goodness has her constantly in hot water.'

'Her honesty for instance, has got us into more than one scrape,' Margaret confided. 'We both did our training at Rome. Once we received a course of lectures from a Doctor who spoke Piedmontese, a dialect which was impossible for anyone to understand. Even the Italian nuns and nurses in the class understood not a word. We dreaded what would happen when we were given the end of lectures examination. Instead of the usual examination however, the Doctor said,

'I'm sure you all understand perfectly all I have told you; I am such a good lecturer,' he boasted, 'therefore I will dispense with the need for an examination. If there is anything you did not understand, please raise your hand.'

Nobody moved except Sister Concepta, whose hand shot up. 'Here comes trouble', I thought resignedly.

'Well?' the Professor smiled, 'What did you not understand?' The Matron, who was sitting behind the Doctor, made frantic signals at Concepta to sit down.

Concepta replied, 'I understood *niente*' – 'nothing!'

'I beg your pardon?' the Professor asked, puzzled. 'What did you not understand?'

'*Niente*,' quavered Concepta again.

The Professor, unable to credit his ears, turned to Matron for help and she quickly interposed.

'Sister did not understand about the Tubercular testing of cows.'

'That was true, as we hadn't understood *anything*,' continued Margaret.

Relieved, the Professor explained in detail. Then, turning to Concepta he again asked, 'Have you understood?' Concepta, rising, answered 'No' but her words were drowned by Matron, 'Yes, yes thank you, Sir', as she shoved his hat into his hand and practically pushed the somewhat bewildered man out of the door.

In spite of their difficulties, Concepta and

Margaret enjoyed Rome. On their day off the two little Sisters explored the Eternal City. The Seat of Christendom had plenty to offer two such ardent tourists. 'We must have seen every Church in Rome,' Concepta once declared.

'I think it was entirely due to Sister Concepta's rigid discipline that I managed to spare any time from sightseeing to attend to my studies,' Margaret told me. 'She would stay up half the night studying and arise again at dawn to continue work. This made me feel guilty as I lay on in bed.' The earnest little scholar had an added burden as she found the language very difficult, whereas Margaret took to it like a duck to water and was soon in animated conversation with everyone she met. More often than not (to Sister Concepta's mild disapproval), the subjects under discussion, far from being professional, were of football or cars – Sister's ruling passions. One of her greatest pleasures was to see a football match on television. Brought up in a family of boys, where football was the *raison d'être*, she naturally had developed an un-nunlike devotion to the sport.

Perhaps in another Convent the Sister would have had to give up her harmless interest in the anatomy of every new car and her admiration for the Napoli Wanderers, but in this congregation the Sisters were encouraged to develop their individual personalities. While their Spiritual life was guided, they were all completely different personalities, with their own individual gifts and hobbies. Sister Francis could enjoy being domesticated and the linen and furniture were a joy to behold, whilst for special meals her sauces were a famed speciality.

Mother Ann's artistic temperament caused her to be teased on many occasions by the other nuns when they mimicked her raptures at the 'line' of a floral arrangement, or the flight of a gull, but they unanimously agreed that no one could paint a spiritual bouquet or arrange a bunch of flowers as she.

Sister Jude's accomplishment was that she was the quickest and neatest knitter of any of the Community and could decipher the most complicated patterns.

Concepta embroidered beautifully. Joan was in her element as Librarian. Patrick scorned any handicraft, except when she did some knitting, which she loathed, to mortify the flesh, yet with her personality uncramped, where would one find a better Public Relations Officer? I wondered.

Then there was Claire, the Convent's odd job man.

'I'm a jack of all trades and master of none,' she told me cheerfully as she mended fuses, repaired cracks in the plaster, or expertly performed a plumbing job.

In spite of the many different types gathered together under one roof, this did not create discord. The nuns had a respect and tolerance for one another's gifts and – that wasn't beyond making sacrifices. Thus Sister Francis, who didn't know a Picasso from a Rembrandt, willingly spent a whole free afternoon trotting beside a rapturous Ann around the Naples Gallery of Paintings. The Sisters never went anywhere alone, even in Ireland; this rule was naturally more strictly adhered to in Naples. Cathleen and I were sometimes roped in as partners. We were always pleased to accompany the nuns as one could never hope for better company. There was Sister Jude, who insisted on bargaining with every street vendor she met. Though she had no intention whatsoever of buying, she liked to show how low she could bring the price. To walk with Patrick meant an introduction to the cream of society at every step.

'That was the little Indian princess who married an Italian last year. It was a very spectacular wedding, the procession even included elephants. She is a charming little person and now speaks Italian beautifully,' and meeting another fashion plate, she told me. 'We also received an invitation to her wedding, it was a very splendid affair,' and she described the wedding and guests. Once when I was out walking with Sister Patrick, a lady who had noted her lady-like air and obvious refinement accompanied by the unfashionable but neat, simple, grey dress and short veil, approached her to ask if 'you would care for a post as governess to my little girl'. Patrick politely explained her situation and the woman departed. Turning to me she said, 'I bet her little cocoa is a little horror if she has actually to go searching the streets for a governess.'

The nuns introduced me to the pleasures of the *'passegiata'* or stroll, which was the Italian national hobby.

The chief pleasure and pastime on these walks, and one which I willingly shared, was gaping. The climate was particularly suited to the occupation. Men and women sat for hours under the umbrellas of pavement cafes and stared at their fellow men. There was always plenty to see and one quickly learned the rules of the game – a passing girl's face, figure and carriage were observed, then her style of dress noted, next her escort appraised as to suitability and in the moment of their passing one 'gave' them a past, present and future, according to the mood of one's imagination.

While all kinds of people indulged in this hobby, those who appeared to have made an occupation of it were the nannies. These women – uniform in their fatness as much as in their starched white aprons – sat under the purple blossom trees in the park and managed to knit, chatter like magpies, observe all the passing parade, while watching to see that little Antonio or Maria was not misbehaving. These children, always immaculate and daintily dressed were like figures in a Victorian portrait. In spite of the rather trying necessity involved in keeping clean and tidy they were not entirely deprived of amusement. The park boasted a hire service where tricycles and toy motor cars could be hired for a modest fee; or greater bliss, these tots, by producing ten lire, could take a ride on a miniature carozza drawn by two white goats! The Luna Park nearby provided a miniature steam engine which, with much puffing and hooting, conveyed its fortunate youngsters through tiny stations, tunnels and countryside which boasted a Red Indian camp. As well as these pleasures the Punch and Judy man was a frequent visitor to this part of the park. The children's small, well-fed, well-scrubbed faces upturned to the stage, provided for the passer-by a fascinating display of absorbed and rapidly changing expressions. There is cherubic little Patrizia who stares intently, eyes round and mouth wide open in wonder, or little fat Pietro, his whole fist stuffed in his mouth to control his paroxysms of laughter or the more serious Claudio who, hugging his sides with delight, only allows himself a wide smile, but the chuckling laughter is spilling from his bright eyes.

The park also housed the Napoli aquarium, where all the strange marine life to be found in the sea around Naples were on display. There were monstrous writhing eels, multi-coloured fish darting through live sea flowers and fish for all the world like Walt Disney birds, flapping their transparent wings. Our favourite case contained the ethereal little sea horse, gracefully drifting to and fro about his maritime business.

I had decided to save the aquarium for the rare dull days. It was a treat which made up for the loss of my beloved sun.

Whether from a swinging seat sipping coffee or strolling along the sea front, there was always something to see. On my 'passegiata', I stepped carefully along the footpath to avoid walking on the fishermen's nets, which were spread to dry on the pavements. Dotted here and there on the pavement, bare-footed, blue jerseyed fishermen sat cross-legged, their rucked-leather faces concentrated as they repaired the tears in the nets. As the sun climbed higher in the sky they would tip their moth-eaten straw hats over their eyes and take their siesta on the pavement as relaxed as though reposing on a foam mattress.

On my walk I would stop to share with a

little boy the diversion of a huge octopus who would *not* stay in his wooden tub. The stall-holder would push him firmly into the tub, but immediately his back was turned Signor Octopus would place one long tentacle on the rim of the tub, followed by another and another. Then while the little boy and I gazed in horrified delight, he would slyly and slimly slither his way onto the pavement, only to be spied by the vendor and again ignominiously replaced. The performance was repeated over and over again to our fascinated delight.

Peddlers selling such commodities as melon, sweets and slices of coconut were a usual sight at Mergellina, though the most colourful peddler was always the balloon man, his multi-coloured balloons floating in a cluster above his head, the resulting splash of colour forming an artist's palette against the vivid blue of the sky. Once I saw a red balloon escape from the bunch. It floated in a perfectly straight line higher and higher into the cloudless sky. I watched as, never veering from its vertical line, it was lost to the naked eye.

CHAPTER 4

NAPOLI NIGHT

When I had been three weeks at the *Regina Maris*, and getting more used to the different techniques and ward routines, Sister Patrick asked me, 'Do you think you could manage a tour of night duty?'

I certainly did not, but remembering my resolution, I replied 'Yes Sister, I could.' Sister Patrick at once became business-like.

'Very good, take tomorrow off duty and report on the ward at 8 p.m. tomorrow night. You work seven consecutive nights followed by a day off. The staff usually do three weeks day duty and one week of night duty per month. If you are worried about anything, simply call our department and I'll be up in a few minutes.' She smiled unexpectedly and said, 'Good luck!'

I needed all the luck in the world next night. Promptly at eight, dressed in my neat uniform and firmly clutching my dictionary, I stood at Sister's desk. Outwardly crisp, calm and professional, my heart was ticking over uncomfortably and I felt slightly sick.

Sister Bernadette greeted me with a warm smile.

'I felt simply awful my first night duty,' she consoled, 'but it gets easier with every night and it is amazing how much Italian you will learn on night duty.'

I began to feel better as she began the night report and later introduced me to my two assistant nurses, Amata and Anna.

Sister left me and I began my duties. It was true one learned an amazing amount on night duty. One learned because one absolutely *had* to learn. 'This is a ghastly way to learn a language,' I thought as I painstakingly laboured over the simplest phrases. After a conversation involving more than one or two sentences I would feel utterly exhausted.

It was on night duty that I became really well acquainted with the four assistant nurses, Amata, Rosario, Anna and Bunions. On my first 'nights' I started duty with Amata and Anna as my assistants. I had already taught them not to shout when I did not understand and so we had already passed the first lesson in our relationship.

They greeted me now with an encouraging and conspiring look. Kissing my cheek Amata announced, 'We will work together in great harmony.' Then Anna, having greeted me in the same manner, they departed together to make the company's beds.

Every Professor who visited the hospital had his own operating team. One Professor might have three assistant doctors and an anaesthetist trailing him around the hospital. Consequently it was not unusual for a patient to be surrounded with four or five doctors all busily prescribing treatment which the poor nurses had to jot down.

Each night, Grimaldi, Ucello and Treves, the three housemen, would take turns at visiting the wards. In the day time they were only responsible for Caracciolo's patients (the other Professors having their own housemen) but at night they were responsible for the whole hospital.

Doctor Grimaldi was on duty my first night on 'nights'. A short, dark man with bright, black eyes and a neat toothbrush moustache, he arrived punctually at 10 p.m. to visit the landing. With meticulous politeness he bowed, presented his compliments and asked if he 'could be of service?' A little stunned by the speech, I asked would he visit the 'gastric' who had a pain. 'With pleasure,' he replied.

He examined the patient thoroughly and found that the pain was not serious and could be relieved with an antacid. Before ordering the medicine, however, Grimaldi gave the patient a true description of his ulcer – 'like the top of Vesuvius', of the normal stomach acid which further irritated 'the crater' and how the alkaline mixture which we were about to administer would neutralize the acid and *'ecco'*, your pain goes too'. The patient and I almost felt like applauding this speech. I did not know then, but I was to learn that Grimaldi always spoke in 'speeches' – words were his joy. He chose them with as much pleasure and artistic satisfaction as a painter mixing his colours. Though these speeches were sometimes exasperating (when one was in a hurry), they were never a bore, and the little doctor was held in affectionate esteem by both patients and staff alike.

Treves, whilst being the most efficient doctor of the trio, had the manner of a particularly fiendish schoolboy. With his white teeth flashing and his dark eyes full of mischief, it was always a cause of amazement to me that he was so good at his profession. He would emerge from the Theatre, having performed a particularly brilliant piece of surgery, and release a white mouse in the midst of the formerly lauding nurses. To my fury he laughed outright at my poor Italian. Once I asked him the diagnosis of a new patient.

'D.S.L.S.,' he replied.

'What does that stand for?'

'Dio Solo lo sa.' He had disappeared down the stairs, a satanical grin on his face, before my laboured Italian translated, 'Dio Solo lo sa' as – 'God alone only knows'.

In spite of Treves' torments, we preferred him to Ucello, the third houseman, who, whilst being a very good and conscientious doctor, had a charming manner as well. He would always come at once when called, and was never bad tempered, no matter what the hour. His personality, despite his virtues, was colourless, and true to the perversity of human nature, it was to the teasing, tormenting Treves, that the staff gave their first love.

On the fourth evening on 'nights', my two assistants were changed and two new assistants commenced their tour of duty. One of them, Rosario – la *regina di Mergellina* – Mergellina's Queen, as she had been christened, was an acknowledged beauty. Child of a Spanish father and an Italian mother, she was a delight. Everything about Rosario was a creation of beauty, her long, shapely limbs, the slim figure with its unbelievably tiny waist, the frail neck supporting her lovely head, with its coils of jet black hair. Her face, with its huge dark eyes, was at once childishly vulnerable and womanly appealing. The fact that her teeth were slightly uneven only crowned her perfection. Rosario knew she was lovely, admired her own flawlessness and enjoyed her universal admiration.

The other girls, instead of feeling jealous

of their colleague, loved her. They would pinch her cheek, kiss their fingers and call her Bella Rosario, because she had been twice blessed by the gods, not only with looks, but an affectionate, unselfish disposition. It was inevitable that among such a romantically-minded crowd of girls, Rosario should be a central figure for match-making. Unfortunately, their queen, their bella Rosario, made one miserable failure after another. She constantly fell for the wrong types and barely gave herself time to convalesce from one hopeless affair when she was in the throes of another.

'*Figlia mia*, give this one up. He is old enough to be your father,' her despairing parents would beg. A few weeks later, '*Carissima*, this one will never offer you marriage, he only wants to boast of his conquests, give him up,' her friends would implore. Rosario, however, continued on her own sweet path of destruction. When I started my fourth evening on night duty with her, she called me aside and ceremoniously showed me a little silver locket.

'This is from Michele. We are madly in love,' and she proceeded to tell how the fabulous Michele could kiss. 'How lovely I'll look as a bride,' she declared, as she gazed with satisfaction at herself in the mirror. 'I'll wear real orange blossom from Sorrento in my hair,' she added, wetting the tip of her finger and flicking her eyebrows.

'Yes, you'll make a fairy-tale bride,' I agreed indulgently. I realized she had again embarked on the precarious vessel of love.

The other assistant nurse was nick-named Bunions, because of her difficult feet. She was one of the most temperamental people with whom I have ever worked. Having worked with her on day duty, I dreaded going on night duty with her as one never knew what her mood would be.

'Yes,' agreed all the 'diplomats', 'she is disagreeable, but her cooking! It is fit for the gods.'

This was true. At midnight, when she had completed her nightly duties, she would retire to the kitchen and commence crashing and banging about as if it were daybreak. I tried coaxing her to make less noise, but interference only made her more temperamental and consequently more noisy. Presently, when the meal was ready, she would yell down the corridor at the pitch of her lungs, 'Sheila, hurry, come quickly', and if I tried to fit in a few more duties before answering the summons, there would be another blood-curdling yell. It was better if one did not want all the patients awake, to come at once.

The table was always laid beautifully. There was another ritual when we sat down. I would take a bite, Bunion watching my face closely. The morsel was then chewed and I would exclaim *'ma e buona'* – 'it is good'. Bunion would nod her satisfaction and we would both eat. Her cooking *was* exquisite. The cheese omelettes or grilled sole, served with asparagus dripping butter sauce, created by Bunion was delectable. Throughout the meal encouragement came from Bunion, *'Mangia, mangia'* – 'Eat, eat, Sheila'. She was genuinely happy when I ate well and not only hurt, but insulted, when I did not.

We needed to eat well on night duty to find energy for the endless duties. In Irish hospitals most treatments and medicines have been given by 10 p.m. Not so in Naples, treatments, injection and medicines were given right around the clock. Many patients were wakened two and three times at night for medicines, or more frequently for injections.

New patients were often surprised when I entered their rooms at night. 'Why Signorina, are you not in bed?' was the common query. I explained that I was the night nurse. 'Yes,' they replied, 'but you go to bed, if we need you we will call you, there is no need to stay awake.' The conception of the night nurse as we know her, on duty to give the same supervision and care at night as during the day, was unknown to them.

One man in a two-bedded room, asked me if I would not rest in the other empty bed, and he would call me if anyone rang. I discovered that some of the patients had known hospitals where there was no supervision at night – hence the very real need for relatives in attendance. When they did discover that not only were there night staff in the *Regina Maris*, but these same Signorinas were anxious to see they were comfortable during the night, to change a rumpled draw sheet, give a thirst-quenching drink, a tablet to relieve a pain, renew a soiled dressing, adjust an uncomfortable bandage or merely to reassure them, their gratitude was quite touching.

I have never cared for night duty. It is an unnatural existence. One eats breakfast at 8 p.m., lunch at midnight and when the rest of mankind is in its deepest slumber at 4a.m., the night nurse is drinking black coffee to prepare for the busiest portion of her watch. Then when the world awakens she goes, weary and grey-faced, to try to sleep amidst the noise and light of day. Yet on 'nights' in Naples there was great compensation in the beauty of the night.

A treat in which I often indulged was to look out of the enormous windows of the *salotto* (the wide portion of the corridor, which formed a large sitting-room). The lights, like diamonds on black velvet, sparkled in a heavy necklace around the margin of the bay. The bed of the ancient lava flow of Vesuvius was also lit at night, outlining this mountain, which at all times dominates the scene. To complete the perfection of the picture, the yacht sails in the harbour were also outlined in lights. When the moon shone on the barely ruffled surface of the Mediterranean, it created a lucid and unbelievably lovely sketch on the dark canvas of night.

I could generally also spare a few moments at dawn, before commencing the early morning routine, to admire the awakening day. The ancient volcanic rock of Vesuvius borrowed colour from the changing sky. From black it subtly altered to purple, then deep blue. Then as the sun crept higher it was crimson, next a soft pink and at the instant of dawn's birth, a glorious gold.

Despite this pleasure, I counted the time until I would be back again on day duty. Sister Francis counted the days with me – 'You are doing fine,' she encouraged, 'Only two more days and the week is over.'

I went to bed on the morning of my fifth night, tired after a very busy time. As I fell asleep the thought ran through my mind: 'Only two more nights to go and my first night duty in Italy will be over.'

I slept well in spite of the bright sunshine and was awakened later by Sister Francis.

'What time it is?' I asked sleepily.

'Five o'clock. I called you because there is

a visitor for you.'

'For *me*. But I know no one.'

'It's a gentleman. Hurry up now. Do yourself up nicely and go into the drawing room. I'll get him a cup of tea.'

Burning with curiosity, I dressed quickly and hurried down to the parlour.

To my surprise it was Neill O'Connor, my seat companion on the plane coming out to Rome. He was attached to NATO and had a few days leave.

'I just had to check that you'd arrived safely. Knowing how susceptible Italian males are to pretty girls...'

Before I had adequately gathered my wits together he had extracted from me a promise not only to show him some of the sights of Naples before I returned on duty, but also, on my first day off, to go with him to the semi-legendary Isle of Capri.

Eight o'clock was just striking as I arrived, panting but in complete uniform at Sister's desk.

'Bless us child, how did you manage to change so quickly?' Sister Ann, who was on duty, asked.

'Practice,' I laughed.

'I didn't expect you on duty for another hour at least, as Sister Anthony told me that you had gone out with your young man.' Then she proceeded to give me the night report.

'No. 16 has improved but will still need careful watching, he can have a mild sedative tonight if necessary. No. 2 comfortable for fasting blood sugar tomorrow,' and she went through the report. 'Good-night Sheila and God bless you,' Sister said as she left the landing. 'If there is anything worrying you be sure to ring down.'

'All right Sister, good night and thank you.' Then I read through my report again, carefully noting which patients would need special watching and listing the treatments due. I gave the assistant nurses the list of night drinks required by the patients. No one drank coffee at night, as all were convinced that it would cause insomnia. A few patients requested weak tea with lemon, but the greater number wanted Camomile tea, an obnoxious brew made from Camomile leaves, which was considered an excellent soporific.

While most Italian patients took far more medicines, pills and injections than their Irish counterparts, there was also a certain number, mostly countryfolk, who were terrified of drugs – for these a cup of Camomile tea was more satisfactory in inducing sleep than a Soneryl tablet.

'The only one likely to be ill,' I thought, 'will be little Antonio.' After his tonsillectary he had a slight haemorrhage. Therefore before doing a round of my patients I first visited the little boy.

The son of a sailor, Toni was in a six-bedded ward, full of children. His parents sat quietly beside his bed. Glancing down the row of beds I saw that each child had a parent sitting attentively by him. This was one of the wards where the director did not wish relatives to stay at night. 'One might as well try to separate a cub from a wolf,' I thought, 'as to get these people to leave.' Like the other night nurses, I did not 'see' the parents in this ward.

The children were all sleeping; Antonio also slept, his lashes spread like fans on his pale face. I checked his pulse rate and was able to reassure his parents, as it was normal. Then, whispering to the adults, I explained that 'I am the night nurse and will be on duty until morning. I will come around regularly during the night, but if there is anything you want, do not be afraid to ring.' They thanked me courteously and I left to attend to my other duties.

I set up sub-cutaneous drips, settled patients for the night, checked blood pressure, pulse and respiration of the cerebral cases and commenced the ten o'clock injections. The tonsil cases were all given coagulant (anti-haemorrhage) injections. Antonio was still sleeping when I had my syringe ready and his buttock bared. I gently wakened him, as I feel that it is less frightening to a child if one explains that he will 'feel a prick' than to be wakened by the sting of an injection given while asleep.

'Antonio, a little prick,' he whimpered for a moment, then went back to sleep. His condition was still satisfactory. When I checked him at eleven however, the pulse had risen ten beats. I 'phoned his doctor, Professor Angelini, who replied, 'Thank you for ringing. Give another coagulant (he named a stronger injection). Watch him carefully and do a quarter-hourly pulse check.'

The next hour was extremely busy. I had to be at the little boy's bedside at fifteen minute intervals and in between times attend to other patients who required attention. I have often noticed when one is anxious about one patient, the whole corridor seems to want attention at that particular time. Tonight was no exception and my little 'Assist' Rosario was run off her feet, answering bells which growled incessantly like rabid dogs. At eleven forty-five, Antonio's pulse had risen another four beats and he spat fresh blood. I immediately called Angelini – 'I'll be there in five minutes,' he replied. Rosario had put the suturing instruments into the sterilizer without having been told. We wrapped the little boy in blankets and carried him to the treatment room. The child at this stage was very trusting and unexcited. If only we could keep him calm, it would help a great deal.

Unfortunately the parents became wildly excited and in spite of our pleas and reassurance the mother became quite hysterical. 'My baby, my baby is dying,' she wailed. Her husband, realizing the damage she could do by frightening the child, also lost his head and started to shout. This brought other curious relatives to their doors who, in an attempt to be helpful, only added to the bedlam. Finally the little boy became frightened with all the hubbub and started to cry and when Angelini arrived he was bleeding freely. Fortunately the Professor was a practical man and a skilled worker. Without ado he quickly banished the wailing relatives. We held the child firmly and he quickly sutured the bleeding points. In fifteen minutes the little one was treated and warmly tucked up in bed again where he was soon sound asleep.

Rosario and I commenced mopping up the treatment room.

The rest of the night was uneventful.

CHAPTER 5

CAPRI

On the appointed day I was ready and waiting in my room long before 8 a.m. Peeping out of the window I saw Neill descend from a taxi at the door. I gathered up my handbag and jacket and flew out to the door. The Sisters, who were just leaving Chapel after Mass, called after me, 'Have a nice time,' 'Visit the Blue Grotto' and 'Don't get sunburned.'

Neill was wearing a *very* gay shirt. I felt a little embarrassed when he caught me staring.

'Don't worry,' he said laughing, 'One must be gay going to Capri.'

'And isn't it a heavenly day?' I added joyfully.

The air was like a good wine and the sky an unbroken canopy of blue. Our little boat ploughed a double furrow of foaming white in the still blueness of the bay, a transparent blueness which changed from shades of sky, aquamarine, turquoise and royal blue, until nearing the island, it was an incredible navy.

Our boat drew slowly into the little bay,

with its rather oriental-looking shops and rows of multi-coloured boats drawn up on the shingle. Capri is a delicious shock to the senses. The white buildings are pristine and gleaming in the intense light, and everywhere there is colour – walls which are blossoms of purple Bougainvillea, green of vines, purple of grapes and the gay colours of orange and lemon trees. The smell is a mixture of sea and foliage, lemons and blossom.

We stepped off the boat onto the white pier where rows of porters in neat uniforms, the names of their hotels on their caps, beseeched us to go to their hotels.

We escaped from these well-meaning young men – from those who wanted to show us the 'best restaurant', 'the best souvenir shops' or take us on a 'quick, cheap tour'. We wanted to do our own exploring.

First we sauntered leisurely around the little shops of the port.

'What would you like?' Neill asked, indicating the wares.

I pretended to think very hard and then announced,

'An apple.'

'A what?'

'A large, luscious, juicy one.'

'I'll do my best.'

In a few seconds we were happily munching.

Neill noticed a motor boat about to depart

for the Blue Grotto. We hailed the boat and stepped in just as it took off. By the time we reached the cave the tide had risen and almost blocked off the entrance. We transferred to a small row-boat and, lying flat on the bottom of the boat, were just able to scrape through. We found ourselves in a weird world of strange shapes and forms. Stalactites and stalagmites hung from the roof and grew from the walls, forming live and twisted shapes. Over and through it all penetrated a shimmering blue light which cast its glow upward from the water. Light poured into the cave from below, giving depth and change to the spectrum of blues in the water. The boatman's oars disturbed shoals of tiny fish, which darted through the water like silver arrows. When we returned to the port, a weather-beaten old islander from his huge old-fashioned open-topped car, asked, 'Taxi?'

'Yes,' Neill answered unexpectedly, and I was bundled in.

'Tour of the island please,' my escort requested.

We took the snaking road upwards to Anacapri. I was enchanted. The road was a switchback of sunny views.

Anacapri is situated in the high part of the island and is connected with Capri by a beautiful panoramic road which offered an unforgettable view of the Gulf of Naples, from the Sorrentine peninsular to the island of Ischia.

'We are now passing San Antonio's Chapel,' lectured our guide.

Below the little Chapel was a staircase hewn in the solid rock, which in ancient times had been the only connection between Anacapri and the Marina Grande. We admired the riot of blossoms and flowers.

'Oh look, Neill, crocuses growing wild, and see the blossom, isn't it exquisite?' I said.

I noticed that our driver/guide, instead of slowing, accelerated going round corners. This hurtled me right across the seat on top of Neill. When I asked our driver, 'Why do you suddenly put on speed going around the bend?' he replied with a cheerful grin – 'I thought you would both like it.'

We stopped at Anacapri – Capri's little jewel set high on the cliffs. The gay little square cried out to be explored, but we were hungry. Our restaurant was a lucky choice. We dined on a sun-lit terrace on fresh lobster salad and drank Soave wine. Drifts of daffodils lit the lawns in front of us while below, groves of cherry, almond and orange blossom stepped to the sea.

After our meal we wandered lazily around Anacapri. Neill noticed in the main square an attractive little building which housed the entrance to a chair lift.

'Would you like to go up?' Neill asked me.

'Where does it go?' I asked the attendant.

'To the highest point on the island, Mount Solaro, 1,932 feet high. A twelve minute ride, Signorina. Here comes a chair, Signorina. Quickly – you wish to go?'

I did. In a second we were both buckled into chairs and riding high above small terraced gardens and orchards. The top of the mountain had been converted into a garden and there was the inevitable bar, with an assortment of coloured umbrellas offering shade to its patrons.

'Shall we return on foot?' I suggested.

'You are energetic,' my companion teased, but he joined me as we plunged down the mountainside, singing on our way. We entered a delightful little valley which a notice informed us was the Valley of Santa Maria a Cetrella. From here a little path, no more than a goat track, beckoned us on. We emerged at a lane which forked to the left and led us to a palatial villa. On the delicate, wrought-iron gates was the name San Michele. So this was the dream villa of the Swedish author-physician Axel Münthe. We wandered around the home of the great author, but it was the gardens which captivated me. Gleaming white pillars, strung with vines, through which one looked down on the sea lined one side, while the gardens were a profusion of colourful and exotic blooms. It was a 'first white days of the world' garden. The white-pillared walk led to a little pagoda which contained the unexpected sight of a sphinx (on which I wished). Then, drugged with sun and wine, we stood in the little pagoda and gazed dreamily down at the little harbour.

'Like Paradise,' murmured Neill, to which I replied,

'That reminds me of the story Sister Ann told me about Capri, which she read in a brochure about the Island. Apparently when God painted the universe, He worked every day until Sunday. Being a true Artist He was unable to repose on this day of rest. Surveying His palette He noticed that He had used all the more sombre colours and soft tints in the northern countries. There remained many very bright and gaudy colours. With his palette knife, He began slapping on pure, unmixed colours to make a sky of cobalt and a sea of ultra-marine, edged with emerald green. His chrome-yellow lit the island with sunshine. The Creator called the masterpiece Capri – and there it is below you.'

My companion smiled. 'What a lovely explanation. I'm inclined to think we have found the land of youth of our ancient Irish ancestors. Yes, they did believe in a land of sunshine and flowers and permanent youth. Do you think Oisin had taken a Mediterranean cruise at some stage?

CHAPTER 6

CALL ME MADAM

Sister Patrick called at my room later that week.

'I came to tell you that there will be a companion for you in four weeks time. Mother Marie has found another Irish nurse who is coming here at the beginning of March. I did not wish to tell you until everything was arranged, but now I have the nurse's confirmation that she will come. Her name is Cathleen Bligh.'

I counted the days until Cathleen's arrival. I looked forward eagerly to the day when I would have a companion with whom to share the joys and trials of life in Naples.

Finally Cathleen arrived. I met a fair, round-faced girl who was still full of high spirits after the long journey which she had travelled over-land. I realized suddenly that I was very lucky to have found such an ideal companion. Cathleen almost expressed my thoughts when she blurted out—

'I'm so pleased you are young and cheerful. I was terrified the only Irish nurse here might be an ancient, with no sense of humour.'

She next began to ply me with questions about the hospital and Naples. I answered to the best of my ability, enjoying my temporary role of 'the old girl'.

'What are the nuns like?' asked Cathleen. 'They certainly gave me a lovely welcome.'

'You will love them,' I replied, 'They are the most kind-hearted, unselfish women I ever met in my life. I never knew such people existed until I came here. Their life is one long sacrifice and yet they are always cheerful.'

'Someone once said, if you want to find the most genuine, cheerful, hearty laughter, look in a Convent.'

'It's true, they are always laughing and playing jokes. They even call Sister Jude, Dennis the Menace, after the mischievous little boy in the strip cartoon. But don't forget,' I added, 'that Jude, for all her fun and games, is a brilliant midwife, who controls the whole Maternity Department, and her proud boast is that her staff help to bring more than 500 babies into the world each year.'

'They have a frightfully high standard of nursing, haven't they?'

'Yes, it must be a combination of fine training and dedication.'

Sister Ann popped her head around the door.

'Sorry, I thought you were out. I noticed

your hands were sore and thought you could use this bottle of lotion. Someone gave it to me, but of course I don't use that sort of stuff.' She smiled and disappeared, having first deposited a bottle of hand cream on my dressing-table.

'See what I mean?' I said to Cathleen. 'That was Sister Ann. She is a perfect angel. At the moment she has no definite department, so she does relief, that means she gets the busiest times on each ward, yet she is always smiling.'

'Yes, they are generous,' she replied, 'Sister Claire gave me a little dish of sugared almonds this morning, just when I felt like a nibble of something sweet.'

Sister Claire and Sister Teresa were generous donors of sugared almonds. They worked in the *nido* or nest, as the baby unit was called. When a baby was christened, the parents distributed dainty dishes of sugared almonds, beautifully wrapped in pink or blue tulle with a little label inscribed with baby's name, weight and date of birth. Sister Claire and Sister Teresa collected one of these without fail, for each little mite in their nest.

Cathleen went on duty on the 2nd landing and I was on the third. There was some controversy among the patients and staff in deciding how we should be addressed. The Italian trained nurses or 'diplomats', were called Signorina Gina or Carla as the case might be. The untrained staff being addressed by their christian names without the prefix. Usually I was called Signorina Sheila, but on occasions Miss Sheila, which I did not like nearly so well. Cathleen and I smiled when we were referred to as the 'misses'. The nuns merely called us Sheila and Cathleen, with the exception of Sister Patrick, who always absentmindedly addressed us by the undeserved title of Sister. My professoressa was very precise about the matter. 'One does not address a lady as just "miss",' she explained seriously to her son, '"Madam" is more correct,' and to me, 'May we call you madam?'

'Certainly,' I replied, suppressing a smile. I remembered the Drury Lane musical 'Call me Madam!'

It made a great difference to me, having another girl with whom I could go on excursions. The Sisters had done their best to prevent my feeling lonely, but their time had been limited. Now we planned what we would do and where we would go together. We planned first to study the language thoroughly and then to really get to know the people and the country. We decided that tourists only get a very superficial idea of the country, especially if they don't know Italian.

'This is a chance in a million and I'm not

going to avail of it,' Cathleen stoutly asserted.

'Yes,' I agreed. 'When we do know Italian, look at the wonderful places we may visit. We must go to Capri together too, it is a gorgeous place.'

'You lucky girl, to have been there, especially 'in luxury style'. I don't think I'll ever catch up on all you know,' she sighed.

Poor Cathleen! Arriving eight weeks after me, I think she thought I spoke fluent Italian already. As I passed on any information the Sisters had given me, I was quite astonished at all they had managed to teach me in such a short space of time.

The three weeks' interval between tours of night duty seemed to pass like lightning. It was my turn again, and I was doing my rounds one night, when there was a power failure. It was a peculiarity of Naples, that quite frequently the electricity broke down for anything from five to fifteen minutes, plunging the whole city in darkness. The Sisters had an emergency supply of candles for these occasions. No sooner had the excitable parente arrived at their doors calling for 'luce', than a lighted candle was quickly thrust into their hands.

During this failure of current, a maternity case arrived in the Hall. The Maternity Department was on the sixth floor, the lift would not function without current, so that Sister Jude had to escort her wailing patient and her lamenting relatives up six flights of stairs by candlelight. The scene was so reminiscent of one of the more melancholy plays at the Abbey Theatre, Dublin, that I found myself for a moment actually diverted and completely immune to its pathos. My momentary lack of compassion was soon perished as the commotion awakened my patients and they commenced an uproar for lights and attention. Added to this, one of the *parente*, inspired by the beautiful night and the romance of candlelight, went out onto his balcony and proceeded to serenade the pretty girl who had an appendicectomy in the room next door.

I was fortunate that with all this commotion I had only one seriously ill patient on my landing – Giuseppi, a little boy who, in trying to obtain a free ride by clinging to the side of a tram, had fallen onto the tram lines, and had his foot mangled by the following tram. Child of a large, poor family, he was at least fortunate that his father's insurance covered his admission to one of our wards. Though dangerously ill and in great pain at times, I marvelled at this little boy's endurance. He thanked us courteously for anything we did for him and frequently reassured his loving relatives. It was a great relief to me to know at the end

93

of my week on night duty, that 'Seppi was at least out of danger. I had been very impressed by the child's courage and the wealth of affection in this otherwise poverty-stricken family.

The Italians' natural affection for their children seemed to have gone to the other extreme among the upper classes. In many cases these children would have benefited from firmer handling. Instead, they were constantly admired, kissed, cuddled and caressed, until they felt themselves the lords of creation. Perhaps this attitude explained the insufferable vanity and petulance of many of the adults. When these spoilt children became patients, it required the patience of Job to deal with them. Even to swallow a tablet involved fits of purple screaming and tantrums, sufficient to daunt the most stout-hearted nurse. When one, employing a little child-psychology, made a friendly approach to the child, perhaps first applying a compress to his teddy bear, and then an equally painless one to his own little forehead, the child would be quite happy with this interesting game, until the over-fond relatives clustered around clucking, 'Oh the poor little angel, how good he is,' – 'Does it hurt?' 'Bear it, darling, and we'll buy you a beautiful gift'.

Naturally the clever little *bambinello* decided to show how much he suffered, and nurse beat a hasty retreat before the display!

On the other hand, the middle class and poor children, though equally loved, (one never heard of a case of cruelty to children in Naples), were far less spoiled. They were generally cared for beautifully. A group of school-going Neapolitan children, boys and girls, in the spotless, dark smocks or white *broderie anglaise* for babies, with different coloured ribbons at their chins to denote their grades, were a bunch of the cleanest, happiest and healthiest little ones to be found anywhere in the world. Their parents could not afford to gratify their every wish, as the wealthy parents could, and this produced a far happier little human. Kissing one another on pudgy, dusky cheeks with true Italian demonstrative affection, they trotted along, hand in hand or arm in arm. This brotherly love and affection did not prevent an odd row breaking out as round-polled warrior schoolboys beat one another over the black skulls with their satchels.

Unless very fortunate or rich, their education was a scanty one. Naples had insufficient schools for the huge population of young people. The authorities were therefore forced to use a shift system, where different groups of children attended schools for a half day or every second day. The children only received half the tuition they would normally get in a more fortunate community. Naturally, in a society where schooling was obtained under such difficulties, if a child did not attend, nobody interfered. There was thus a stratum which was completely illiterate, never having received any formal education. These neglected children ran bare-footed around the streets of Naples or clung, barnacle fashion, to the backs of the trams, looking for mischief, or some way to pick up a few surplus lire or a meal to supplement the rather inadequate home diet. Many of these children grew up completely illiterate and speaking a dialect only understood in the precincts of Naples. Despite these handicaps, many became excellent workmen, or fishermen, and the girls made the world's finest wives. Still, it was natural that many of these young boys, with no one to direct their energies and possessing a high degree of intelligence, should devote most of their time to mischief and later, when hunger gnawed, to crime. They developed into the famed character, typical only to Naples, the *Scugnizzi*, groups of adolescents who scratched a living from the crumbs of crime.

There existed dire poverty in Naples, as in all great cities. Contrary to popular stories and opinion, this poverty was not accompanied by depression, despair and mournful faces. The temperament of the people would not allow such unalloyed sorrow. The poorest homes sang the latest *canzone* with gusto. Gossip was exchanged in shrill voices across the narrow streets and one was never far from laughter. Even the tiny tots playing in the gutter, the soft contours of whose little bottoms were exposed to the four winds, might be under-nourished, but they were far from unhappy. Their innocent, angelic faces showed only childish absorption as they made a *pizza* of the mud, and childish bliss when they planked this same pie on the head of their nearest companion.

Even in the poorest hovel, there was always an attempt at brightness, even if it only meant the blue and gold of the Madonna's picture, or the sharp red, luxurious blossom of a geranium grown in the sun. Then there was always also the spontaneous gaiety of a permanent bunting display, a flag day caused by the daily wash strung right across the streets overhead, as the multi-coloured assortment of these huge family washes decorated the alleys. No doubt that immediately after the War the suffering of the poor in this beautiful city was appalling. Foreign aid improved social schemes, an awakening public conscience and the unselfish work of the famous Father Borrelli and now the English Father Scott James, in providing homes for the *Scugnizzi* has done much to improve the city since those times.

I once saw three very young *Scugnizzi*

pinning a patch into a very tattered jacket for a member of their clan. I watched with pity which quickly changed to amusement as the little chap, on seeing me watching, put on an act for my benefit. In perfect authenticity he mimed a very grand fellow being fitted by his tailor. He primped and posed and stuck out his chest, while his two 'fitters' played the parts of the two fussy tailors to perfection. I thought 'the show' worth a fifty lira piece, which I held out to them: one approached cautiously, grabbed the coin, flashed a white smile and then they took to their heels and ran.

Once, when Sister Bernadette was on night duty, she was gazing out the window at the stars. The streets were deserted save for two women, who, with long brooms made of twigs, were sweeping away the rubbish of the day. Some newspapers, stirred by the wind, lifted and moved in a corner of the street. Then she perceived that the newspapers were not being stirred by the wind, but by four little boys, who were sleeping on the hard pavement, the papers being their inadequate bedding. Bernadette's heart went out in pity to the little outlaws. She collected the bread and cheese intended for her supper and brought it down to the boys. 'When I approached with the food they were terrified,' she told us later. 'I had to reassure them over and over again that I meant them no harm and didn't intend to have them locked up anywhere.' Finally like deer they took the food and ran. 'I wonder whether I did right to bring the food to them. I only supplied one meal and now they will be afraid to come back to sleep there and though uncomfortable, at least it was sheltered.' I remembered her words this night duty. On glancing out the window, I saw a young boy at the angle of a stone wall, climb into a cardboard box, curl up like a puppy and go to sleep. Undisturbed, he lived in his cardboard home for over a week before he moved on.

CHAPTER 7

SAINT PATRICK'S DAY

One day, looking at the calendar quite casually, I noticed that St. Patrick's day was creeping up on us almost unawares and I exclaimed aloud.

'Che gioia,' said Cathleen in her enthusiasm, rushing to the wardrobe to see what she would wear. She slipped into an attractive beige model, but found to her dismay that the dress would not fasten. In her enthusiasm for spaghetti, she had added a few unwanted pounds. 'Tomorrow I start a diet,' she declared firmly.

Though Cathleen kept rigidly to her diet for a few days, there was no noticeable improvement. She had a healthy appetite and was working exceptionally hard, so after a few days of eating vegetables and fruit, while watching those around her tucking into risottos, *sufflés* and pasta, her resolve was undermined. I came into the dining room to find her expertly and happily forking up a huge plate of spaghetti. She smiled contentedly at me, her chin beautifully stained with tomato sauce.

'I've had the greatest luck,' she said. 'The gallstones from Sicily left me a gift of a length of material, so I needn't diet. Thank heaven,' she added, 'as next week is St. Patrick's day and I couldn't bear to be dieting at a party.'

As I did my work on St. Patrick's day, I was constantly interrupted for *'Auguri'*, or greetings, on this our national feast day. They wished me 'One hundred of these days' and 'May you obtain everything your heart desires'. The warm-hearted, if over enthusiastic embraces of the *ragazze* and parente, rendered me quite breathless at times. Enveloped in the affectionate embrace of a fat Neapolitan woman was like being smothered in a sorbo-rubber mattress. The hand-kissing of the men was more restrained, if equally time-consuming, as the gesture was always accompanied by a flowery speech in which Irish people were pictured half with their eyes cast upwards, the other half with eyes downcast – 'the island of saints and scholars'.

In every room I was offered sweet cakes and light wine or 'orzata', a drink made from almonds. Our barber, Signor Esposito, shyly presented me with a box of sweets to honour the occasion. Some weeks previously, Antonetta had asked my opinion of the barber and I had replied that I considered him a decent type. Now he was stammering his thanks for the 'recommendation'. I could not recall having recommended the barber to anyone, until he said, 'and now Antonetta is my fiancée.' Not wishing to be responsible for any fickle Neapolitan's affair of the heart, I quickly changed the subject.

'Esposito – I have seen your name in many places here. Are you a member of an extremely big family?' I queried.

'Bigger than you think,' he chuckled and proceeded to explain. 'Long ago in Naples, there was a home for unwanted and abandoned babies. The name of the professor in charge of the home was Esposito, so each child was given the surname Esposito. Therefore most of the Espositos you see in Naples today are descendants of those children, as I am,' he finished, quite undaunted that the indiscretion of one of his ancestors was the cause of his proud surname.

The Italians were always delighted with an excuse for a celebration. There was to be a party at the hospital this evening in honour of Saint Patrick. Every nurse I met that morning kissed me soundly on both cheeks and wished me a happy feast day. I was very touched to receive two lovely bouquets of flowers from the nurses and *regazze*. During our afternoon break, I treated them to coffee and cakes, a traditional celebration treat for any special occasion. We sat on the pavement seats under gay striped umbrellas, sipping our black coffee and eating '*dolci*', taking turns to play requests on the juke-box and *thoroughly* enjoying ourselves. That was one of the many qualities I admired in the Italians, their blessed ability to extract the utmost enjoyment from the smallest treat. It was a contagious enjoyment and I always looked forward to our outings together.

The hospital boasted a coffee bar and restaurant, primarily for the convenience of patients' relatives. The coffee bar was a favourite rendezvous for medical and nursing staff and it had the added advantage of non-profit making charges. (One was presented with a small bill at the end of the month).

The dance was held in the coffee bar and was a very lively affair. Cathleen and I wore lovely harp badges, which the nuns had presented to us. Many of the staff wore shamrock!

'These Italians are more Irish than the Gaels themselves,' I thought.

The effect was heightened when Treves came over to me and in faultless Gaelic, asked for the next dance. He had asked one of the Sisters to teach him the phrase and had been practising all the day.

Most of our partners were far below the dancing standard of Irishmen, but they could rival them with 'the gift of the gab'.

These black-eyed Romeos, without the advantage of a Blarney stone, impressed us considerably with their eloquence.

I noticed that the two hospital porters, Gabriel and Stefano, had also been invited to the party. They stood together at the door (seemingly unable to leave their accustomed place of service), and clapped their hands gaily to the music.

Gabriel, better known as 'the archangel', was a huge man, with a small, black moustache and a permanent grin. Dressed in a bright blue boiler suit, he padded around the hospital. As odd-job man, he was responsible for the boilers which supplied the building with hot water as well as for any odd repairs. Another of his duties was to swab down the main staircase daily, a job which was not too tedious, as the stairs were of clean marble and generally the heat evaporated any puddles Gabriel left behind. It was an inexplicable curiosity that Gabriel preferred to swab the stairs from the bottom upwards, instead of from above downwards. Sister Patrick tried to reason with him, but in vain. One day, as usual, she found Gabriel at his usual 'below-up' method. Sister Patrick believed that the way to treat a Neapolitan servant was to use their own method of expression, to shout, rant and rave. The gentle rebuke was utterly useless here. Taking a deep breath she started the usual tirade. Suddenly she lost her breath and began to choke. Coughing and red-faced, she was led by the archangel into the bar. He sat her down on a chair, fed her a glass of water and solicitously patted her on the shoulder. 'There, there, gently, gently Matron,' he consoled, until Patrick, lungs reventilated, returned to her duties, deciding to leave the high angel to his own devices for the present. This porter had 'a weakness for the drink', as Sister Francis would say. If a patient tipped him over-generously for carrying his luggage downstairs, Gabriel would celebrate in the boiler room. This meant that either we had no hot water that day, as he let the fire go out, or that Gabriel, having stoked the fire so well before his binge, the hot taps were nearly ready to explode as they gushed forth steam and boiling water.

His assistant, Stefano, tried to cover up for Gabriel's mistakes. Stefano was a living skeleton. Even a vulture would have sniffed at his long, thin frame. He walked with a limp and his badly-matched glass eye did not add to his appearance. The first time I saw this pathetic creature I took him for a patient. Certainly he looked much more ill than most of the people occupying beds on the landing. 'Who is he?' I asked Bernadette, and she replied. 'After the war there were so many invalids in Italy that the Government made a decree that for every so many men an Italian employs, he must also employ one invalid.' Stefano could therefore have collected his weekly pay packet with little if any justification. That was not so however, for Stefano was certainly no parasite on his community. He did all in his power to justify his place on the staff. He posted letters, went on errands, and was constantly on the move, doing the small, light jobs needed to relieve the more able-bodied people for other duties. Even now, I noticed at the party, he was still being helpful. I watched him unobtrusively remove empty glasses or change a record on the gramophone.

Throughout the dance we were served with numerous trays of dainty sandwiches and mouth-watering tiny cakes. The only beverages paraded however were all alcoholic. 'Spumante' – the Italian champagne, wines, whiskies, brandies and sherries all flowed freely. The doctors and nurses, used to wine since babyhood, drank glass after glass with enjoyment. I had never enjoyed more than one glass of sherry or champagne. Therefore I found myself having to refuse the numerous drinks pressed upon me, and I could see that I was hurting the feelings of my hosts.

Finally I hit upon the solution. The archangel was standing by the door watching the merry-making. I caught his eye and indicated my glass. 'You like' – 'Yes', he liked. From then on, every drink I was offered, I accepted gratefully, and unobtrusively passed it on to Gabriel, the porter. The staff were most anxious that I should feel welcome, and consequently the glasses of yellow, amber, gold and ruby liquor were brought to me in rapid succession. Suddenly to my horror, there was a tremendous crash and my gallant Archangel slid ungracefully to the floor, where he reposed, a seraphic grin on his face. The fallen angel was out for the count.

CHAPTER 8

THEATRE SONG

One day I came off duty at five o'clock and went into Cathleen's room.

'I've had a foul day,' she greeted me, 'Two of our nurses are at home with 'flu, so I was on alone for the afternoon with five cases for theatre, and we had two partial gastrectomies yesterday and *both* are playing up today. We've spent the last half an hour pumping cardiac and respiratory stimulants into one of them, who collapsed. He is all right now, thank God, but I'm utterly exhausted.' Then seeing my woe-begone face, she asked. 'What happened to you?'

'The worst day since I came here,' I answered. 'You know we too are short-staffed with the 'flu,' I explained. 'Now we have the heaviest assortment of cases you ever saw. Five are cases of Lorenzotti's (the brain surgeon), on hourly control charts and intra venous drips. Barely has one attended to one patient, when it is time to do the next. Then there is Caracciolo's abdomino-perineal of yesterday on continuous suction and at least a dozen fresh major ops. On top of this we have the most excitable crowd of relatives you ever saw in your life! They run out on the corridor and grab hold of my arms as I rush past, shouting an unintelligible gabble at me. Today was one of those days when I couldn't understand *anything*, so that they could have been asking for a glass of water, or telling me their relative had collapsed for all I knew.' I had felt like Hans Anderson's mermaid in the fairytale, their hands reaching out for me was like the seaweed trying to catch the mermaid. 'Finally I checked one of Lorenzotti's cases and found his blood pressure way up in the skies, and when I tried to tell Treves, I was so tired and upset that my Italian was *terrible*. He couldn't understand a word and just stood there grinning insufferably, while I became more and more agitated. Then he said, 'Calmly, calmly Sheila, I have not understood'. I just caught him by the shoulders and shook him to *make* him understand. This made him laugh, so at this final indignity I burst into tears.'

'You poor thing,' said Cathleen, 'I know just how you feel. I had a howling fit last week and felt *such* a baby after it.'

'That's just it, I don't know how I'll face them tomorrow after making such a fool of myself. After all, Treves was very decent not to get mad at my shaking him like a rat.'

'We'll go out and have a marsala and forget it all. Let us be like the Italians and switch our emotions in a moment,' Cathleen cheered me.

'We can't go out – have you seen the sky?'

The sky was a malevolent purple, lit by an eerie orange glow. The normally mirror-glass bay, rolled restlessly as though shaken by violent indigestion. We were about to have one of our rare but wonderful electric storms. The streets were deserted.

'Let's defy all the conventions,' Cathleen suggested, 'and go out.'

'Yes,' I was persuaded. 'The weather is a perfect reflection of my feelings, and it is ages since I felt the rain on my face.'

Though still early afternoon when we left the hospital, it was pitch dark. The air felt close and sultry. Suddenly there was a blinding flash of lightning which lit Vesuvius and the sea for a second. This was followed by another and another, nature's fireworks display in a lightning storm to rival any human effort. Then there was the military roll of deafening thunder. Slowly and carefully the big heavy drops began to fall, followed quite suddenly by the emptying of the heavenly reservoir. The rain came in one huge torrent, without apparent separation between drops. Gasping and laughing we were mercilessly showered, our hair plastered to our heads, faces streaming water, wet to the skin, we exulted in the elements. Adding to our joy, was the startled expression of amazement on the faces of Neapolitans who, glancing out of their windows, saw two drowned rats actually *enjoying* this ghastly weather. Squelching in our sodden footwear we returned happily to the hospital cleansed by the elements of our former depression. Calm and contented again, I commenced to tackle my problem in a realistic and sensible manner. Before I went to bed that night, I had mastered the imperative mood and learned two new sentences which Sister Claire helped me to compose – 'I will come to you when I have completed my present task' and 'The matter is urgent. Please come at once, doctor'.

'Very useful sentences,' I thought, as I drifted off to dreamland.

My very next evening duty I had cause to employ my second sentence. 'The matter is urgent, please come at once, doctor'.

A nine months old baby boy, who had been admitted an hour previously for observation queried intestinal obstruction had vomited and was now screaming in pain, his little knees drawn tightly up over his tummy. The Paediatrician, Professor Gambuti, always left one of his assistants in the hospital. They were all very keen, alert young men, therefore, I had only opened my mouth to say 'Doctor, the baby in four–' when he asked, 'Colic?'

'Yes,' I replied, and he hurried to the room in time to examine the baby during an attack of pain, and to feel the sausage-shaped tumor which confirmed the diagnosis of Intus-susception. This condition is the telescoping of one piece of bowel into another, and when it occurs the little patient is more often than not, a bonny baby boy.

I knew the condition was very serious and that the earlier the operation was carried out the greater the chance of a successful result. When the assistant doctor 'phoned his Professor the reply he heard was the expected one: 'Make all preparations for immediate operation. I will come at once.' I informed Sister Bernadette, who alerted the theatre staff. She then helped me to prepare the little boy quickly for the theatre. When the professor arrived fifteen minutes later, the baby was already in theatre, bound with cotton wool and loose crepe bandage like an infant Christ to the little wooden cross used for abdominal operation of babies. A few minutes palpation of the child's abdomen, a few terse questions and answers and the professor was 'scrubbing-up' and the anaesthetist beginning the induction of anaesthesia.

The operation began. The professor, as usual, described the various stages to his team of doctors.

When the gut was exposed it was clear that the simple expedient of reduction by squeezing out the telescoped piece of gut could not be employed. The 'telescope' had nipped the blood supply long enough to cause the beginning of gangrene. The affected portion of gut would have to be completely cut out and the two ends rejoined. The baby, already shocked from pain, would have to withstand a major surgical procedure. The team worked in silence, the only sounds being the clap of instruments into rubber gloves and the chink of used instruments as they were discarded. Quickly and deftly the surgeon removed the gangrenous piece of gut and performed an 'anastomosis' or 'joining together' of the remaining pieces. His assistants worked feverishly, anticipating the surgeon's wants regarding instruments, clipping off exposed blood-vessels with artery forceps, and keeping the field of operation clean and free of blood to enable the Professor to work quickly. Co-operation between the team was essential, as the less time the abdomen was left exposed and the child was under general anaesthesia, the better would be his chance of recovery.

The anaesthetist, with his own serious responsibilities, was anxiously watching the child's condition. He noted with concern the rapid, shallow movement of the air bag which corresponded exactly with the rhythm of the patient's breathing. Adjusting the gases on his machine, he placed his stethoscope to the child's small chest. The brave little heart beat a rapid though weak tattoo, like the terrified heart of a caged bird. The anaesthetist, a highly skilled man at his profession, had previously exposed one of the child's veins and inserted a special needle which was closed with a minute valve. This forethought saved time, and now in this emergency when the cardiac system showed signs of collapse, he was able, without any delay, to inject a drug which would help the heart keep up. Though the baby's condition was critical throughout, he rallied again after the injection and it seemed that the doctors would win their fight.

The greater part of the operation had been completed when the anaesthetist suddenly alerted the team that the child had collapsed. He did not respond to a further stimulant injected into the vein. The breathing bag was suddenly appallingly still and the small portion of the baby's face below the mask was pinched, white and shrunken. The Professor, with commendable alacrity, began to massage the tiny heart. There was no response. Tension mounted in the theatre as the anaesthetist injected a mixture of adrenaline and coramine directly into the heart, and the Professor continued the massage. The anaesthetist besought the Professor with his eyes – 'Any change?' but the surgeon only shook his head and responded gruffly, *'Niente'* – 'Nothing.' After another minute, which dragged like an hour, Professor

Gambuti stated, 'I think I felt a slight tremor of the heart muscle', and then with a little note of excitement in his voice, 'Yes, I did'.

'Continue, Sir, continue the massage,' urged the anaesthetist, in his concern moving his own hand in the squeeze-relax, squeeze-relax movement the professor was employing. While the anaesthetist prepared an intravenous fluid drip, the surgeon hopefully continued the massage. The watchers, who had been observing as though hypnotised, the muscles of the professor's forearm contract-relax, contract-relax in harmony with the squeeze-relax, squeeze-relax movement of his fingers hidden inside the child's small chest cavity, noted at once when the arm was suddenly still. At the same time they also saw the relaxation of the concentrated contracted muscles surrounding his eyes. The surgeon's eyes opened wide, he tilted his head to one side as though listening, then gave a great sigh of relief.

'It's fluttering,' he announced, then, 'It's moving,' and, after another few seconds, 'Very rapid, but beating regularly.'

The whole emergency had lasted less than five minutes, yet the worry of those minutes had made them stretch into an eternity. The Professor's long drawn sigh was echoed around the theatre.

During this critical period the great man's assistants worked quickly and quietly to prepare and have to hand every conceivable aid their master would demand. The most junior member of the team could only stand tense, unable to help because the others were sufficient to handle the crisis. His was the greater strain, as the other doctors all had a duty to perform to keep their minds occupied. At last his tension released itself, and as his master and assistants closed the wound, Sister Margaret, who was 'scrubbed' for the case, was astonished as the young Italian burst into song. He sang 'Grenada' with verve and vitality in a magnificent tenor.

The Professor looked up as he put in a final clip, 'Brava, brava', he said enthusiastically. The eyes of the assistants smiled warmly over their masks. They still stood grouped around the little figure on the cross, the anaesthetist administering oxygen with a tiny mask. The little one would remain in theatre until it gained more strength to be moved to the landing.

'Sing!' requested the Professor, and the doctor again filled the theatre with his magnificent voice.

The nuns, dining in a room below, heard the splendid voice and traced it to the theatre. They stood outside listening. It was a still, silent evening, the very air seemed to amplify the clear voice and to carry it into the furthermost corners of the hospital. Parente tip-toed quietly away from their charges and formed an enthusiastic audience outside the theatre. Then a few patients drifted along to swell the crowd. They stood around with bandaged heads and limbs in plaster of paris, putting their fingers to their lips to invoke silence, that the singer might not be disturbed or the spell broken. There was a swish of rubber tyres on marble and a patient in a wheel chair was added to the throng. Lastly, the nurses, who had resisted temptation until they could hold out no longer, arrived like a flutter of white moths. The crowd of nuns, patients and nurses, like children who would be punished if they betrayed their presence, made a comical picture as they tried to restrain themselves from enthusiastic applause.

Their cup was full when the singer broke into Gounod's beautiful 'Ave Maria'. The voice soared in purity – 'Et benedictus fructus ventris tui Jesus.'

'Sancta Maria, Mater Dei–'

The baby awakened and cried 'ba-bo' – his daddy.

With uninterrupted joy the singer finished his song to his final thankful 'Amen'.

'Any child would prefer to listen to you than to the choirs of angels, young man,' the Professor chuckled, as he left the theatre to follow the baby to the ward, his arm placed affectionately around the shoulders of his youngest house surgeon.

CHAPTER 9

...AND NOT A DROP TO DRINK

Throughout the spring, which was quite warm in Naples, the Neapolitans clung tenaciously to their woollen vests, heavy topcoats and huge mufflers. Gradually though, as the days grew longer and warmer, these garments were slowly discarded and Naples became even more gay as her inhabitants changed into the bright raiment of Summer.

By June, lessons were now becoming rather a trial to us as the weather became hotter. It was necessary to hurry off duty, take a crowded tram into the city to Tina (Dr. Treves' fiancée and our new teacher's) house, while the other nurses back at the *Regina Maris* went for a refreshing swim. We barely had time for our lesson, the return rush and a quick cup of coffee before going back on duty. Our day was such a hectic rush, that as the weather grew warmer, we were quite exhausted by eventide and only ready for bed.

One particularly hot afternoon I was on duty with Gina, a girl with a very lovely face but the temper of an alley-cat. We had a difference of opinion and she threw her usual tantrum which generally had the effect of terrifying me. On this occasion my temper had been frayed with the heat, and before I realized it, I was using my tongue in a delightful exchange of insults. We were brawling like fishwives. Quite suddenly I thought that this was shocking behaviour, and in the same moment realized that we had been quarrelling in Italian. Whoops! I must know the language to be able to quarrel in it. With a change of emotions quite understandable to my former opponent, I said quite cheerfully.

'I'm getting very good at Italian.'

'You are Sheila, you speak it just like an Italian.'

We embraced.

'Which would you prefer to do, the temps. or the treatments?' I asked.

'I'll do the temps. if you do the treatments,' she answered peacefully.

A short time later there was a sibilant hiss from the kitchen.

'Coffee, Sheila?' Gina asked.

'*Si*, with pleasure.'

We celebrated our unspoken peace pact over two sweet, black coffees. My ability to defend myself had raised me high in her esteem.

That evening I telephoned Tina to cancel any further lessons. She was as pleased as I, as her family wished to go to the mountains and Tina had meant to stay in sultry Naples, as her impeccable manners would not permit her to cancel our lessons!

By August most of the wealthy people of Naples had left the sweltering city for the cool of the mountains. The heat was now quite unbearable.

'From now on,' Sister Joan informed us, 'we will only have emergency operations, others will either wait for the cooler season or go to hospitals in cooler regions. If we are lucky we should have very few patients shortly.'

Unfortunately we were not lucky. The flow of patients continued uninterrupted and, as they were mostly emergencies, they were more difficult cases and more tiring for us.

The clammy heat drained our energy and in the afternoons even to walk was an effort. Not a stir of wind broke the dead heat. Clothes stuck, feet were swollen and heads ached from the glare. Everyone who could lie down in the afternoon for the *siesta* did so. We usually worked every second afternoon and having had a sleep the afternoon before, one felt almost drunk at the same hour when on duty next day.

Certainly I felt sympathy for Maria and Lucia, when Sister Bernadette returned one evening to find their work undone and the pair fast asleep in the treatment room.

In this tormenting heat a daily swim would have meant bliss to us, but alas, one had to pay the equivalent of five to seven shillings for a swim at Naples. We therefore only took occasional bathes as a treat. Once Cathleen and I went swimming at a less expensive 'sea-garden' as the strips of beaches were called. When we swam fifty yards from the shore, we found ourselves embalmed from head to toe in waste oil from the harbour's ships. Though we saved a small sum, it took a full week to remove the oil from our hair.

When sea-bathing was so expensive, it was fortunate that an ordinary bath was so pleasant at the hospital. As the bathroom which I used was situated on the corridor exactly opposite the Chapel, it was constantly being used as a storage room for flowers, until the nuns had time to arrange them. The Sisters rarely bought the blooms which were used to decorate the altar. They usually arrived as gifts from grateful patients or were sent from relatives of patients in the hospital. The maternity floor was a particularly generous donor as the arrival of the stork was always synonymous with the arrival of baskets and vases of magnificent blooms. When one celebrated lady produced a son and heir, the Chapel was drenched with the exquisite perfume of one hundred and twenty blush-pink orchids!

I enjoyed taking my bath in a room containing vases and baskets of lovely flowers. True, there might be the slight inconvenience of removing a few dozen long-stemmed roses from the bath before I washed, but that was nothing to the luxury of soaking in a warm bath surrounded with the richest and rarest of blooms.

As I washed away the cares of the day my imagination would cloak me in the guise of a Prima donna in her dressing room, surrounded by the tokens of esteem of her noble admirers. I sang happily as I reflected on the performance I had given as 'Madame Butterfly' last night. The Prince had told me my soul-stirring rendering of 'One Fine Day' had brought tears to his eyes. My gaze rested for a moment on the Prince's basket – the usual red roses. There was a little orange blossom tree in a tub from the Honourable E. who had vowed to die in exile if I should refuse him. Those beautiful silvery flowers were from the renowned De Salis brothers who, I think, had fought a duel over me.

My reflections as a Prima donna were in no way disturbed by my tuneless singing of the latest Italian hit tunes, or by the fact that the good St. Louis nuns of my schooldays had so often admonished me to 'just open and close your mouth' on the high notes!

When our week's night duty came around

we were pleased.

'We will be working in the cool of the night and sleeping during this awful heat,' said Cathleen.

What we had not bargained for was the fact that it was virtually impossible to sleep during the day.

Bathed in sweat we tossed and turned, unable to sleep. Eventually we gave up the effort. Exhaustion lent us two or three hours sleep during the day, the remaining time we spent on leisurely walks along the sea-front and in the vicinity of the hospital.

One morning in one of these streets a little man in pyjamas stepped out of his window on to his balcony overlooking the street and with a rope he lowered his basket. A little boy came out of the coffee shop below and put a roll and cup of coffee in the basket. Then the old boy carefully hauled up his breakfast.

In the height of this heat wave the reservoir supplying the whole city broke down.

There was no water for washing. We felt clammy and uncomfortable and the patients complained bitterly, refusing even to acknowledge that we had no 'acqua'.

'I never realized how much we depend on water,' said Lucia, in the dining room, as we sipped our *latte caffe*. 'Isn't it horrible to have to come to breakfast without a wash and not be able even to clean one's teeth.'

'Cathleen and I washed with cologne,' I explained.

'I wondered why you smelled like a bad anaesthetic,' Lucia grinned.

On duty the patients grumbled bitterly when hot and feverish, they could not be washed. The smell of Eau de Cologne became quite overpowering as staff and patients tried to find a substitute for soap and water. All operations were cancelled, and the fittest patients discharged. Every task became twice as difficult. When we 'scrubbed up', it was to use the same bowl of disinfectant water over and over again, followed by rinsing in alcohol, a process designed to peel the skin off our hands. An emergency system brought water from outlying districts to be sold in the city, but the ration was quite inadequate. The sultry heat, aided and abetted by the psychological effect of hearing the same word over and over again, water, water, water, added to our torture by developing in all of us an unquenchable thirst. *'Ho sete'* – I thirst, was the constant cry. The odd bottle of distilled water supplied by the hospital, together with the lemonade which we bought with our own money, only helped a little.

The days wore on and still there was no sign of a break. We were assured by the 'powers that be' that everything possible was being done to repair the damage with all speed. No doubt they were rushing the job, with hotels and shops crying that their tourists were leaving in droves because of the situation. One poor hotel proprietor in an effort to give satisfaction to an important visitor, had used bottled water to the value of twenty pounds to supply his bath. Industry was at a standstill as the city waited anxiously for the repair to be completed.

'I declare the place is beginning to 'pong'. The sinks are smelly and as for the *gabinetti!*' Lucia declared as we did our morning round of bed-making.

'I hardly think so, Lucia,' I replied. 'Look at all the buckets of disinfectant we are using.'

'Disinfectant is no substitute for the water carriage system,' she replied, darkly significant.

'Let's hope this one will be a bit understanding about the linen situation,' I sighed as we entered the next room.

The patients were used to having daily changes of bed linen. With the laundry out of action this was now quite impossible, as the supply of linen could never last out. We had no way of knowing *when* the water would return and in the meantime we had to economise to allow really necessary changes.

Our patient was not co-operative.

'I must have clean linen today.'

'But we gave you clean linen only yesterday.'

'I have been in this bed 24 hours and I have a fever; I must be changed.'

'Signora, I understand how you feel, but you must know that there is no water,' and so on, the long tiresome explanations by weary nurses to disgruntled patients.

'I'll lose my patience if this keeps up,' declared Lucia. 'Cheer up, Cathleen and I have enough money for a swim for the three of us. We will chance spending it on a good dip this evening and hope that by tomorrow all will be well.'

The next day, the fifth day of our thirst, all was *not* well. In fact where Cathleen and I were concerned it was worse. Our finances had dwindled to the princely sum of fifty lira – about sevenpence, with which we bought a large bottle of mineral water.

'If it's not back tomorrow, we will have to resort to intra-venous fluids' we decided when we retired for the night.

I was awakened during the night by a great noise as of rushing torrents. It *was* rushing torrents – the water taps all over the hospital had been turned on during the drought and now, like Moses' rock, they all gushed water. It was back again – very much so. When I rushed out into the corridor in my dressing gown to join the Sisters and nurses, we were met by a beautiful waterfall, sliding down the stairs. Some patients had left plugs in their sinks and the water had overflowed. Our lovely marble-floored hospital was rapidly turning into another little Venice. The nurses, sisters, two doctors and a few relatives were all sloshing around merrily like ducks in the wet, when Sister Patrick appeared, resplendent in a pair of galoshes. The unexpected appearance of galoshes in Naples struck some of those present as hilariously funny and a ripple of delighted giggles broke out, until Sister Patrick spoke sternly.

'Sisters and nurses, I have been informed that the water will last only one hour. We have already wasted thirty minutes – so to work, get all the buckets you can find, plug in all baths and sinks and fill every receptacle you can find. We must have water tomorrow. No one is to take a drink of tap water, it may not be safe.'

As usual our organizing general had thought of everything. We set to work with a will, and, by the time the water was again cut off, we had filled every container in the hospital. Then the fun began as, with mops and pails, we slopped around in an attempt to soak up some of the water. We managed to improve the situation a little in spite of the 'help' rendered by our two housemen, who, when they weren't trying to flick water down our necks, or throwing wet floor cloths at one another, were upsetting the buckets in an attempt to elude capture. At 2 a.m. the *Regina Maris* had suddenly become more noisy than Puck Fair, as we whooped and laughed and splashed like a group of school kids. Sister Ann called from the ward kitchen in perfect Neapolitan style, 'P-s-s-s-s, *scugnizzi*, come and get it!' We were handed large cups of hot coffee after which the 'party' broke up and we returned to our beds.

CHAPTER 10

MOUNTAIN INTERLUDE

I awoke one morning in July feeling slightly queasy.

'You'll feel better after your coffee,' Cathleen assured me.

That morning I learned the Italian phrase for 'My stomach turns,' and a little later from the semi-comfort of my bed I was giving vent to all the new expressions of dolour I had learned from my patients.

'I'll never eat another bite as long as I live,' I vowed, holding my poor tormented middle. We promptly dubbed the malady 'Italian tummy'. It wasn't long until Cathleen also succumbed. The Sisters waited on us hand and foot. Their patience was extraordinary with the two querulous patients who refused every dainty tit-bit with which the poor Sisters tried to tempt their appetites.

In three days we lost the extra pounds which we had gained from pasta eating, our eyes were blue-shadowed and our healthy tans had turned a sickly yellow. Listlessly we went back on duty. Though we were sufficiently recovered, we felt tired and we were more easily irritated by our patients.

Sister Patrick passed me on the stairs one morning, looking me up and down with a frown and then asked abruptly, 'Have you been vomiting?'

'No,' I replied.

Then she poked Cathleen's ribs, 'Too thin,' and left us.

We laughed, 'The 'misses' must look glamorous this morning.'

That evening Mother David came into the dining room where Cathleen and I were silently poking bits of spaghetti around our plates.

'Sister Bernadette and Sister Claire are having supplies sent up to them tomorrow.' These two Sisters were at present enjoying a few days leave at the nuns' little flat in the mountains, which they used in turn for their vacation each year. 'They sent a letter to say they were starving,' Mother continued, 'I can't understand it, really, as Sister Patrick said she left a fully stocked larder and they are only there three days. Still they are young and the Rivisondoli air certainly gives one a good appetite. That's why you two are to bring up the supplies. You can stay the week-end.'

'Oh, Mother, that's wonderful,' we gasped, hardly able to believe our ears.

Our tiredness momentarily deserted us as

we rushed around collecting our needs for three days, 'where the weather would be cool'.

One of the most lovable traits of the Sisters, was that always our happiness was their happiness. Now, with sparkling eyes, they helped us to get ready, while whetting our enthusiasm with descriptions of the joys to come.

'The people are just like Irish country folk,' said Sister Francis, and this was the ultimate in praise coming from her.

'The cheese!' said Sister Concepta rapturously, and she kissed her fingers in the Italian style.

But the scenery, they all assured us, was 'beyond compare'.

Next morning, as we were leaving, the whole community gathered at the top of our flight of steps to wish us God speed and to deliver messages to the other two holiday-makers whom we were to join. The nuns unconsciously imitated some of the Italian customers. Seeing us off now, as if we were going to the ends of the earth was typically Italian, but it made the departure more exciting. It was even more fun when they pretended to be *really* Latin and became emotional at our departure.

The heat of the day had already reached furnace pitch, as, loaded down with parcels of food, we squashed into the train which took us the first lap of our journey. Fortunately we had our 'bus seats booked, as there were twice the amount of passengers which the vehicle should hold. We sank gratefully into our seats.

A few minutes later a woman and her son arrived and sat down on the two seats opposite us. After a few seconds the woman asked if we would mind changing seats with her. She muttered some vague reason. 'Certainly,' we agreed and settled down again. Hardly were we seated when we were disturbed by two blazing women – 'These were *their* seats we were sitting on, they had booked their seats, etc., etc.' The conductor was called and he started to shout at us also. 'You can't take a booked seat–You can't ride on the 'bus without a seat,' he harangued.

'Those two crooks,' Cathleen said to me in English, 'They swapped seats with us without having booked one themselves.'

We turned to our previous dispossessors and angrily told them in no uncertain terms, what we thought of them and ordered them to give us back our seats. Stunned that we spoke the language so well, they gave them up quickly and departed. We were muttering angrily to one another about the meanness of people who would play such a trick on foreigners, who could not speak their language, when we looked around the 'bus. Everyone was smiling approvingly at us.

'You speak the language very well,' one matron beamed.

'Where are you from?' demanded another, 'America?'

'No,' we replied briefly.

English?'

'No.'

'German?'

The others joined in. 'They are fair. Norway perhaps?'

'No.'

'*Dove?*– Where?' – everyone was interested in this little game.

Finally we gave in– 'Irish', we stated proudly.

'Ah, Ireland!' they all exclaimed, and beamed.

The Italians are aware that they have many traits, both good and bad, in common with the Irish and this engenders a warm fellow feeling.

'The beautiful green land,' they state, to show they appreciate our country is also beautiful. 'We are exactly alike,' they assured us. 'Very good Catholics, good sailors and farmers, and we love our families and country and homeland.'

'The Irish have a passion for the music like us,' said another.

'They eat and drink well,' said another with appreciation.

'And their women are home-makers and

good-lookers,' put in a weather-beaten old man. This was greeted with loud applause.

With such obvious goodwill and friendship being lavished on us, we had to forget the impression made by the seat snatchers as we joined in the banter.

'What do you think of the Italian people?' a young man asked.

'The women are the most beautiful I have ever seen,' I replied sincerely. 'They are kind, lovable and born homemakers.'

The women in the 'bus preened themselves and beamed.

'And the men?' demanded our young man, prepared to be flattered.

'Oh they are strong, handsome, conceited cocks,' I replied, and all the women laughed as the men's faces fell.

With the chatter and laughter, we had not noticed that we were gradually leaving the suburbs of Naples behind and gradually edging out into open country. Now all that we could see were green fields, buffalo-drawn carts and long-skirted, bare-footed peasant women carrying their burdens on their heads. We passed fields of corn and ripening maize, olives and maple trees. The vines climbed up the olive and maple trees and their branches hung in graceful festoons from one tree to another. The fertile land was producing three crops at once. Here and there sun-tanned women worked in the fields. We watched the flat, hot countryside for a while, but gradually succumbed to the enervating heat and dropped into a doze.

I awoke and glanced idly out of the window, only to awake Cathleen quickly.

'You can't miss this,' I said.

Our 'bus had wound high up the mountains and we looked down on glorious tree-clad valleys and rushing streams. Occasionally we passed fairy tale villages perched flightily on the cone of a mountain.

'The air is cooler,' exulted Cathleen.

Yes, one could already feel a stir in the air and it was definitely fresher. Higher and higher wound our 'bus through rich meadows and forests of pine. Finally four thousand feet above sea level we stopped at the little mountain village of Roccaraso. Once a very popular resort, it was practically wiped out by mines in 1943. Now rebuilt, it was obviously quite a popular tourist resort, judging by the attractive hotels and shops. The village gained, we hopped off the 'bus and were met by a jubilant pair of nuns. As usual there was plenty to say.

'I rang Mother yesterday about the food,' began Claire. 'Someone said "Mother, Claire is on the 'phone", and then there was silence as my call time ticked slowly by. Apparently Mother had forgotten I wasn't still at the hospital and thought I was ringing from the 5th floor, so I only had time to say

135

that we had no food, and she replied that she would send you with it, when we were cut off.'

Cathleen ventured, 'How did you manage to clean out the larder in two days?'

'There wasn't anything in the larder to clean out,' Sister Bernadette replied indignantly. 'Sister Concepta gave away everything before she left. Rosa (our neighbour) told us she gave the bread and butter to the hermit, the sugar to the old woman who lives in the cave, and the rest to the Barlotte children.'

'Sister Concepta is a Saint,' sighed Sister Claire, 'She'd give away our bedding if she could get away with it.'

As we were talking, we were tramping across the fields to our village which 'isn't a bit touristy' Bernadette assured us proudly.

'No wonder,' puffed Claire. 'Tourists don't usually fancy a three mile walk at the end of their journey. Well there it is ahead.'

We looked. Crazily suspended on the side of a mountain, our little village with its odd-shaped houses, church spire, and narrow, cobbled streets, looked part of the evening sky. The air was fresh and exquisitely cool.

The nun's summer house was another great pleasure in store. There were four bedrooms, a sitting room, bathroom and kitchen – ideal. From every window there were perfect views of the five mile valley, Roccorasso in the distance and tree clad mountains.

We were having tea when we heard a faint tinkling of bells in the distance. Both nuns jumped up from the table and ran to the window where we joined them. It was the nightly ritual of the cows coming home from pasture. They came alone or in groups from all corners of the valley, the bells around their necks tinkling as they walked. The animals formed one steady stream as they reached the village, each knew his own home, and would find his way to it without any human aid. It was a domestic scene of peaceful tranquility.

Later I went for a walk alone. It was the first time in eight months that I had been able to be out alone after dark and it was an exquisitely exciting experience. Like a newly released prisoner I savoured the freedom. In solitude I walked to the tip of the village, taking huge gulps of the iced air. The only sound was the movements of the cattle in their mangers under the houses. Fireflies flickered and shone like stars, miniature replicas of the galaxy above. The villagers were already asleep in order to be ready for their early start in the fields next morning. I heard snores issuing from some of the open windows.

'It's so peaceful up here,' I exclaimed, on my return.

'Fortunately Margaret and Jude are not

here, or you wouldn't call it peaceful. One never knows what that pair will think of next. The last time Margaret was here she led the Community miles across country to some health springs she had discovered. We walked miles and miles and even crawled through brambles. Joan was going mad over her stockings getting laddered. When we got there, it was a foul cess-pool. I'll never forget how we all stood, torn and scratched and muddy gazing at the stinking slime, with Margaret laughing her head off. I can tell you, the charity of the missionaries was sorely tried. It was with great difficulty we refrained from dropping one of our Community in the cess-pool.'

'Remember the swing she found, in the wood?' recalled Sister Claire. 'We went for a walk in the woods one day together and sat down to read our books. I had a very good "life" of St. Joseph, so I didn't notice anything until Margaret called, "Like a swing, Claire?" as she sailed blissfully back and forth on a home-made swing. Well I was tempted and I fell. I sat in that swing, Margaret pushed, and I was off. Higher and higher I went and it was lovely. Alas, I'm a lot heavier than Margaret. There was an ominous crack and I thought all my bones were broken when I hit the ground. "Speak to me Claire, oh speak to me", wailed Margaret, but, completely winded, I couldn't reply. Then she began to wail and worry about what Mother would say, breaking into Italian in her anxiety. *"Oh Madonna mia cosa farò?* – Mother will kill me. It was all my fault etc., etc." She was so relieved when I "recovered" that she offered to take my cooking day as well as her own.'

'An offer you probably refused?' interposed Bernadette.

'I certainly did.' Apparently the Sisters, when on holiday at Rivisondoli, took turns at being cook. They each had their special dish and could all produce a creditable meal – all except Margaret. Sister Francis used to say that Margaret 'could burn water'. With their usual diplomacy Margaret's day was usually Friday, a fast day anyway.

'We are certainly lucky with our choice of cooks,' declared Cathleen, as she bit into her pancakes. We ate a delicious supper of savoury pancakes followed by the famous delicacy, fresh *Rivisondoli mozzarella*, an exquisite soft buffalo cheese.

'Now pardners, let's have a little music,' announced Bernadette, in a mock 'wild-west' voice. She opened a cupboard and produced an old-fashioned gramophone and we had a gay selection of cowboy tunes as we did the washing up. When the little dining room and kitchen were tidied the Sisters, always industrious, produced their work, Claire her knitting, and Bernadette a bottle and cloth, with which she set to work dry-cleaning their habits. They had put a long-playing record of the 'My Fair Lady' musical on the gramophone before settling down to work. This record was a very popular one with the nuns. On feast days Reverend Mother allowed them to listen to this music. To them it was as good as a seat at the theatre, as they sat during mending and darning their habits and listening to the young girl who 'could have danced all night' and her professor who grew 'accustomed to her face'.

Both Sister Margaret, who had entered the convent soon after leaving school, and Sister Patrick, who could tell of many an evening at Drury Lane, enjoyed the delightful story and music.

Sister Bernadette recounted how, on one free day she noticed Reverend Mother looking around her small community – Mother Ann was busy with a miniature painting of the bay, another group were playing cards, and others were immersed in the world of literature. Only Margaret seemed outside the circle, lost in a world of her own. Mother was concerned as she watched the usually gay one staring at a blank wall, her lips moving. 'She called me and said, "Margaret seems lonely. See if you can help." I had to laugh,' she continued, 'when I discovered that Margaret had learned the whole of "My Fair Lady" by heart, and was reciting it to herself. She was called upon to prove her skill, and would you believe it,' finished Claire, 'before the bell rang for prayers, she had given a one-nun performance of the complete show from beginning to end!'

'Not to mention the encores,' added Bernadette, with a reminiscent chuckle.

'Sleep late tomorrow and have a good rest,' we were warned, as we went to our bedrooms. But the following morning we were up with the sun.

'I had the best sleep of my life,' carolled Cathleen.

'Wasn't it heaven to sleep between blankets again?' I rejoiced.

We spent the week-end exploring the countryside – hiking in the green pine-walled valleys and climbing the nearby hills. Our lunches were eaten in the 'great outdoors' so that we quickly regained our lost colour, and as we faced each meal with colossal appetites after the fresh air and exercise, it was not surprising that we regained our lost weight.

The brief sojourn renewed our flagging vitality and we returned to the *Regina Maris*, our high spirits completely restored.

CHAPTER 11

FOOD FOR A FISHERMAN

One day, when preparing the theatre cases for operation, there appeared to be one man missing. The patient, a fisherman, for hernia operation, seemed to have completely disappeared.

Doctor Grimaldi always did rounds before Professor Caracciolo arrived to operate. He gave the routine pre-anaesthetic examination and ordered the pre-operative drugs. Today when he called, I was rather embarrassed to admit that I had not succeeded in locating the missing man.

'Let me know when he returns and I'll tell him where he gets off. I'll deal with this one who insults our illustrious professor by leaving before his operation, not to mention the insult to my humble self,' and Grimaldi continued with a tirade against the unfortunate man, which was quite fascinating in its eloquence. As usual he became almost lost in appreciation of his own speech and the crime grew in enormity as the words flowed from him.

Finally the young culprit returned. Grimaldi was called and the patient and I awaited him in the treatment room. I confess I waited with a certain amount of anticipation for the show. The rest of the staff also slipped quietly into the room. Grimaldi's speeches were famous and deserved a hearing. The young man, unconcerned, complimented each of us on her beauty as he awaited execution. The girls, always ready to accept flattery, giggled delightedly as this Romeo assured them that if the other fishermen but knew of the youth, grace and loveliness that cared for them in the hospital, we would have the fleet clamouring to have their appendixes out!

Finally Grimaldi arrived and surveyed his audience with appreciation. With suitable severity he demanded,

'Now, sir, explain yourself. Where were you?'

'I went out for a meal.'

'You *what?* Before your operation?'

'Yes dear doctor, I might die under this operation, you understand? I did not want to die unhappy. How could I die happy if I were *hungry?*'

Round one to our fisherman. All the Italians appreciated the importance of one's appetite.

Ignoring his opponent's victory, Grimaldi continued,

'*Fool*, to eat before a surgical intervention

– what did you have?'

A look of remembered ecstasy came into the patient's face. He was back again at the restaurant, a good one, naturally, for perhaps his last meal. Soft music played in the background as mentally he tucked the serviette under his chin.

'I began with a little *Stracciatella.*' Everyone liked Stracciatella, tasty, light broth with egg yolks beaten up in semolina and grated cheese. There was a general sigh of approval.

'Exquisite,' breathed Rosario.

'Magnificent,' said Anna.

'What joy!' breathed Carla.

Grimaldi said nothing but licked his lips,

'Next I ordered *Maccheroni Pnincipe di Napoli.*'

'A princely choice indeed,' enthused Carla, 'Maccheroni with mozzarella cheese, chicken breasts, peas and meat sauce, mmmm,' her ecstatic expression proclaimed her opinion of this choice of dish.

Everyone including the doctor sighed their appreciation. Grimaldi, suddenly realizing that he was playing understudy to the star, recollecting himself, bellowed, 'You eat *Maccheroni Pnincipe di Napoli!* What colossal foolishness. Anything else?'

'Next,' continued our gourmand, 'I enjoyed a *Cappon Magro* – the Queen of Salads.'

I knew this dish, which is made of several

144

layers of boiled vegetables with hard biscuits rubbed with garlic and an anchovy sauce. It also contains egg yolks, pine kernels, capers, parsley and pulped olives, and the whole mixture is sieved and then oil and vinegar are added. On the pyramid formed by the various layers, boiled fish and lobsters in green sauce are arranged.

'Then I had *attorta*.'

'*Attorta!*' Rosario rubbed her little, flat tummy. How she loved the cake made of twisted pastry, with its filling of mouth-watering toasted almonds, chocolate and candied fruit.

'The best,' sang Grimaldi, holding up his thumb and third finger in the familiar Neapolitan gesture of approval. Then leaning forward, his eyes narrowed, he demanded, 'Some cheese? Surely you had a bit of cheese to crown the meal?'

A nod of assent from the fisherman.

'Which one?' Grimaldi demanded impatiently – 'Which one?'

'A *mozzarella* – a fresh *buffalo* cheese from Rivisondali.'

We all approved of this delicacy. Then Rosario asked,

'Did you have fruit?'

'The healthy man must always close the repast with a little fruit,' replied our patient. 'I chose a peach, a ripe fruit, still warm and heavy with the sunshine it had trapped, and flowing over with juice. A perfect peach,' he said, and smiled boldly at Rosario.

'Magnificent choice! Had you coffee afterwards?'

'Yes, no cappucinos for me! I had a short, black coffee, hot as hell, black as night and sweet – (his teeth flashed) as love.'

'But the wine, Signore?' demanded Grimaldi, in agony that this bacchanalian repast should be desecrated with the wrong wine.

But the sailor was an artist, 'A *Valpolicelli*,' he replied.

'Brave, brave, brave!' cried his audience.

CHAPTER 12

JUAN AND GIOVANNI

As the months passed in Italy, Cathleen and I became quite *blasé* about the difficulties of nursing in a foreign land. Even night duty which we had formerly dreaded because of the demands it made on our grasp of the language was no longer the ordeal it had been at first.

In spite of our new-found independence I did feel slightly apprehensive as I went on duty for my week in October. I knew this tour of night duty would be busy as, apart from the usual surgical cases, we had two young men who were dangerously ill.

Juan, a Spanish boy holidaying with his uncle, a doctor, at Ischia, had crashed his car while recklessly driving in an attempt to be back in Naples in time for an opera for which he had booked at the San Carlo, and had sustained serious head injuries, for which he had undergone an operation two days previously. The brain surgeon, whilst battling valiantly for his life, held little if any hope for his chances. His parents had come immediately from Spain to watch by his bedside.

147

The other seriously ill patient was a nine-teen-year-old gardener who had developed acute abdominal pain seven days previously. His relatives had nursed him at home for two days before calling in Professor Caracciolo. The Professor had operated and found a perforated appendix, which should have been urgently treated two days previously.

When I reached the landing this evening, Sister said, 'You are going to be very busy. I'm afraid Juan and Giovanni are both on the danger list. Professor Caracciolo has just arrived to visit Giovanni.'

Caracciolo went in to visit his patient. When he came out his face was grave. When the large group of relatives formed a frightened circle around him, the Professor spoke sadly but briefly.

'We are doing all we can for him, but there is little hope. He is showing no signs of recovery. Giovanni is in God's hands now.'

'Will we take him home?' Giovanni's brother, as spokesman, asked.

'I leave the decision to you,' the Professor answered.

I had been listening in the background. Upset, I turned to Sister Bernadette.

'But why, Sister? Why consider moving a dying man? Surely he could be allowed to die in peace?'

Sister sadly replied, 'I too hate to see him disturbed, but dying patients are practically all taken home at once, here. You see, it's like this,' she continued explaining, 'In Italy, when a dead person is carried through a village (on their way home for burial), a huge tax is levied, so that if a person died in Naples and had to be brought through a few villages on the way to his home town, it would cost his family a fortune, which, after the great cost of hospital treatment here, they can't afford.'

'Why not bury them here in Naples?' I asked.

'A country person would never do that. They have the same strong family feeling for their dead as for their living. Each family has their own burial place and it is there that they are all put to rest. To circumvent this problem,' she added, 'I heard that in a *certain* clinic, they once dressed up the corpse complete with collar and tie, sat him between two relatives in a car, and drove rapidly home. When they arrived home the corpse collapsed and died!'

I was relieved to discover that the relatives had decided to leave Giovanni at the hospital. Their spokesman said, 'If we take him home he will die, but if we leave him here there might be a faint hope for him.'

The Professor gave instructions for the patient to Treves and departed, having left him in his care.

I had barely time to re-read the report and

make my list of night drugs and medicines before the telephone rang to admit a new patient. Administration told me to admit her to Room 22 – a room very much in the luxury class and reserved for very important or very rich people.

'She is under the care of Professor X and her condition is grave,' administration informed me, and my heart sank, as I already had my hands full with Juan and Giovanni.

'Who is Professor X?' I asked Rosario and the house-man Ucello, who were in the treatment room.

'He is the town's greatest financier,' replied Ucello sourly.

'He never had a case here yet that he didn't call in someone else to do his work for him. I bet he couldn't let a boil if he tried.'

This Professor certainly did not appear popular, I mused, as I prepared the room for my new admission.

She arrived on a stretcher, a young woman accompanied by her husband, an elderly, affluent-looking being beside her. I helped her into bed, thinking that she certainly did not look seriously ill. I checked her pulse and found it was perfectly normal. She told me that she and her husband were taking a cruise on their yacht, when after her dinner she had felt ill and been sick. 'I thought it was the lobster, but Gino,' nodding towards her husband, 'insisted that I should see a doctor. He *adores* me,' she simpered.

'And I was right *cara mia*. See, the Professor says that this is a serious condition,' he explained to me, 'He called the ambulance himself and stayed to assist my wife off the yacht. Ah, here he is.' He rose, bowed respectfully and greeted the Professor, who had entered the room as he spoke. The Professor bowed and shook hands, then rushing to the bedside he gushed, 'And the *cara Signora*, how glad I am to see you safely in hospital.' With the utmost politeness he asked permission to palpate the woman's abdomen and proceeded to do so with a face grave and concentrated. Finally he straightened and, drawing his finger tips together, he cleared his throat.

'Could I speak to you for a few moments, outside?' he addressed the husband.

I stayed with the patient, who was beginning to look anxious, and chatted to her to distract her attention from the serious voices outside the door. Then her husband returned unaccompanied and explained. 'The Professor has decided to have a consultation with another colleague. Learned though he is, he wishes his diagnosis confirmed before making any decision. There is modesty for you!'

When X returned, he had a small, red-haired squirrel-like doctor in tow. 'This is my eminent colleague Professor Blah,' he said, introducing the squirrel. Blah went to one side of the bed, X to the other. They each took a wrist and for an interminable time counted the pulse. They examined the abdomen, giving each other long, stern, knowing looks. 'If the woman wasn't nervous before, she will be now,' I thought, annoyed. We were not finished yet. X, explaining to the husband that an operation was necessary, declared that he would not countenance any risks, and that he would call in a physician to check the lady's general health. Within half an hour, not only was there a physician in the room, but also a pathologist, cross-matching blood, an electrocardiagraph operator, making a graph of the heart, and a radiographer, with portable equipment to take X-rays. When an anaesthetist appeared, also wishing to examine the woman, the place looked like an all-Ireland hurling final.

I was run off my feet, fetching and carrying for this bevy of medical men.

'What is her temperature, Signorina?'

'38, Sir,' I replied.

'And the blood pressure?'

'One hundred and twenty over eighty.'

'Urine?'

'Specific gravity 1010, reaction acid, albumen nil, sugar nil,' I read off from my report.

'Her weight?'

'Sorry Sir, I did not weigh her.' 'How

could I have weighed a stretcher case?' I thought sourly.

The pathologist wanted coagulants and alcohol, wool and needles.

The electrocardiagraph operator wanted jelly and salt.

The physician wanted stethoscope, sphygmomanometer and patella hammer. All they lacked was an ophthalmic surgeon.

Responsible for thirty patients, I could hardly supply the requirements of one. Utterly frustrated, I was about to 'phone the Sisters for help, when Sister Patrick appeared.

'Has he driven you mad yet, Sister?'

'Practically Sister,' I replied. 'I have yet to prepare her for immediate operation and I have hardly even seen Juan and Giovanni, let alone the rest of the patients.'

'Very good, I'll call Concepta and she and I will get the patient ready for theatre, while you catch up on your other work.'

I thanked her and visited first Giovanni, then Juan. Both their conditions were critical and I felt very sorry for the Italian and Spanish families, both united in sorrow.

The remarkable difference between the Italian and the Spaniard was demonstrated in the deportment of the two families. Giovanni's relatives crowded around his bed and day or night, they never left his side. They wept and sobbed, openly showing their distress, while the parents of the Spaniard in the room opposite, sat dry-eyed by their dying son. Both parents suffered the same torment, but at least the Italians had the relief of allowing their emotions expression.

Rosario and I changed Giovanni, treated his pressure areas, which were getting sore from lying almost lifeless in the one position. Then we sponged his hands and face and I put up the drip containing at least a dozen different drugs, all arrows in the battle for survival. The distressing part about nursing Giovanni was that, although fully conscious, he had not even the strength to show expression in his eyes: dull and lifeless, they stared into space.

We left him a little more comfortable than formerly, and I hurried around the other patients, attending to their various needs for the night. Knowing than Juan would take more time than the others, I had purposely left him until last.

The Spanish boy was a splendid specimen of young manhood, a veritable Adonis. Fair, tall and well developed, his accident had not yet affected his powerful physique. There was absolutely no indication that he would recover. Everything I recorded in my control pointed to this fact: his scorching temperature, the blood pressure sky high, and his rapid short breaths, which spoke of paralysis of the diaphragm. Yet, every nurse or doctor has seen at least one miracle, and they are always ready to hope for another. When all hope has reasonably failed, and the motor of life is petering out, the human mechanic has always his remembered miracle to prevent despair.

On our landing that night, we required more than one miracle. At one o'clock Giovanni collapsed. His pulse could not be felt. Treves, who had stayed up with his patient, fought desperately for his life. Sadly I dispatched Rosario to 'phone Sister Patrick as I scurried back and forth with requirements for the doctor. 'Subito, subito' – 'quickly, quickly,' ordered the little, dark doctor, his hands deft. Anxiously trying to anticipate his wants, I carried intravenous fluids, coramine, methedrine and oxygen to the bedside. In a corner of the room one of the Sisters, in answer to our 'phone call, was preparing a small altar. The priest entered the room. Sister and I turned back the clothes at the foot of the bed. All in the room knelt as the young man was given the last sacraments. By this time he was unconscious. With an ineffective and almost tender gesture, Treves tucked the blankets around his patient's chin.

'Continue all treatment, including the stimulants, and let me know if you should need me,' he said, and left.

When X's patient came back from theatre

at 2 a.m., I helped the theatre nurse put her to bed.

'What did they do?' I asked.

'Removed a fibroid. I will admit it was an enormous thing,' she admitted grudgingly, 'and that she is better without it, but why it had to be done as an emergency, I don't know. Keeping us up until one at night, when we are starting at six tomorrow, is ridiculous for an operation that could be done during the week.' The theatre nurse left, grumbling under her breath.

I checked the woman's pulse, respiration and blood pressure, then left her in Anna's care while I visited the other patients on the landing, who had been unavoidably neglected this night. Suddenly the bell over Juan's door began to ring urgently. I hurried to the bedside where his mother exclaimed, 'I think he's worse!' She was right. The rapid respirations could now barely be counted. I used the electric suction apparatus to clear the air passages of mucus and assist breathing, but with no noticeable improvement. When I checked the boy's temperature it had increased to 105°, while his pulse had increased in volume, but was slower in rate. These signs and symptoms all indicated a great disimprovement. I called Professor Lorenzotti, the brain surgeon and told him that there was a change for the worse in his patient.

'Give E–' He named a drug for lowering the temperature, 'continue the ice-bags, keep up the nasal suction, give continuous oxygen, and I'll be there within ten minutes.'

Ten minutes later, when the Professor arrived, our Juan was dead. That magnificent golden body would struggle no longer.

Two of the Sisters came to look after the relatives. Anna and Rosario, having served the relatives, insisted that I should have a cup of coffee. We all felt keenly our defeat in the battle against death. Thinking of death reminded me that I had not seen Giovanni for over an hour.

When I went into the room, I noticed at once that there was something different about the patient, and then quickly understood that it was the dreadful sound of his choking, stertorous breathing, that was missing. 'Oh no,' I thought horrified, 'not two–' No, as I reached the bed I could hear Giovanni's breathing, soft, deep and regular, the natural respirations of sleep! I felt his forehead, which was cool and without disturbing his refreshing sleep, my fingers found his pulse. I smiled with pleasure – it was almost normal. I had obtained my 'miracle' after all. The boy's father, seeing me smile, questioned with his eyes, 'How is he?'

I replied, my voice alight with pleasure more keenly felt perhaps because of our previous despair, 'He is going to be all right.'

157

That sentence in any language, is the loveliest I know. For doctors and nurses it atones for all the back-breaking labour, heartbreak and defeats which they must endure, and for the patient's relatives it brings peace after fear.

'He is going to be all right,' Papa repeated to Mama. 'He is going to be all right,' Mama echoed incredulously. The rest of the family, who were sleeping uncomfortably in various corners of the room, awoke, and they too echoed the cry. I was soon in the midst of a jubilant family, who kissed, wept and embraced, chanting 'Giovanni is going to be all right.'

I too came in for my share of kisses. When I disentangled myself, warned them not to wake the patient, and left the room, Giovanni's father stopped me on the corridor and whispered, 'How is the young one across the way?'

'Dead,' I whispered sadly.

He stood for a moment, lost in deep thought, then he walked over to the window where Juan's father stood, looking suddenly very tired and very old. Wordlessly the Italian offered the Spaniard a cigarette, lit it for him, then took one himself. Then, gazing out the window, the two men stood in silence, shoulder to shoulder, watching the dawn of another beautiful day.

CHAPTER 13

NATALE

Signs of Christmas were now to be seen everywhere. A beautiful Christmas tree stood in the hall and outside my room there was a lovely crib. When the nuns first came to Naples, they built their representation of the crib as they had always seen it at home. It contained the figures of the Holy Family, an ox and an ass. When they saw the patients and relatives queuing up to see it they put the fact down to exceptional reverence and were much gratified. In actual fact, the people were very amused at a crib with only three figures, and were queuing to see for themselves 'the peculiar crib of the Irish Sisters'.

The Neapolitan crib was a work of art. Not only did it contain the actual stable, but the whole village of Bethlehem was there, True, often one had to search for the central figures, yet they included in their village every possible tradesman and person likely to be in a village. The baker was there, carrying loaves of fresh-baked bread and what looked like a pizza, also included is the butcher, with his meat, the fruit vendor and the farmer. Those who were not hurrying towards the manger plied their daily trades. The shoemaker mended his shoes, even a woman bathing a child was represented.

These cribs, many of them now important antiques, are brought out every year in the churches.

One of the hospital doctors had taken pity on the Sisters' plight, and after that first Christmas they had a crib to please the most discriminating eye – complete with pizza-maker and washerwoman. Our crib was beautifully lit with concealed lighting, which brilliantly illuminated the Holy Child and parents, while the spectators were left in partial shadow. The artist responsible for the lighting was our wine-soaked Archangel.

On my way to duty I met the said angel on the stairs, and congratulated him. He waved my praises aside, *'niente niente'* – 'nothing, nothing – Gabriel is a person of many talents', he added in self-appreciation, as he continued his journey downstairs.

Sister Patrick's voice drew him up. 'Where are you off to now, Gabriel?' she demanded. 'To the lavatory,' he replied with perfect *sang-froid*, leaving her for once at a loss.

After duty I went into Cathleen's room to find her looking a bit glum. She explained – 'I went shopping with two of the midwives, and as I was passing Upims, I caught sight of our reflections in a shop window. I was appalled at how awful I looked compared with them. I nearly cried.'

I understood perfectly. Only the previous day, one of the Assistants had said to me – 'You foreigners don't care how you look as long as you are comfortable.' 'But they can't be comfortable,' I said to console her.

'I don't care,' she replied, 'I want to look *'elegante'* too. I'll have a dress made, I'll need it for Rivisondoli.' (We had now made up our minds we were going there).

'I'll have one too,' I agreed. 'We can afford it with some of the extra money we received. December's pay can cover our hotel bill.'

Now that we had decided to have an Italian outfit, we had great excitement. The stuff had to be bought, the dressmaker called and the pattern chosen. This is not done in an afternoon in Naples! As usual there is a ritual. Rosario and Anna kindly came with me to buy my material. We went from shop to shop, comparing prices and fingering materials. They decided we wanted a soft blue material. The shop-keeper drew down bale upon bale of blue until the counter was littered. Suddenly Rosario turned to Anna and said, 'But her eyes are green.'

Anna turned and stared at me – 'No, grey.'

The salesman peered. 'They are blue,' he said firmly.

'Green,' said Rosario.

'Grey,' insisted Anna.

The salesman turned and called 'Peppi, come here.' Another salesman appeared.

'What colour are the signorina's eyes?'

We all waited expectantly. I was interested too!

Peppi peered – 'Green, with little islands of…'

'All right, all right,' interrupted the first salesman testily, 'start handing down those bales of green material.'

The nuns went on long Retreats during Christmastide. They also had to prepare gifts and woollens which they knitted and sewed for the many poor families which looked to the nuns for charity. Advent they considered a time of recollection and prayer, so they received no letters from the outside world during these six weeks. When I sympathized with Sister Joan, she said, 'It is a very little sacrifice and think of the pleasure we have when we open all our post at once on Christmas day!'

Cathleen and I promptly decided to do the same, and save our post. We knew we would not have the will-power to refrain from peeping ourselves, so we told Sister Jude, who was 'postman', to give them to Reverend Mother for us, to be saved with those of the other Sisters. They understood perfectly the pleasure of anticipation but teased us, calling us the new postulants.

Unlike the Sisters though, the 'new postulants' found plenty of time for pleasure. Although we were saving our money, we did not find it too expensive to re-visit the island of Ischia. We had often visited this little island in the bay of Naples during the summer, as it afforded very good beaches for swimming. We could cross on the workmen's ferry, which was much less expensive than the usual tourist steamer. In December we again crossed by ferry. The green island was now a blaze of colour as the vine leaves were autumn-tinted in shades of gold, orange, red and brown. In between the vineyards dotted all over the island, were the tangerine trees loaded with Christmas oranges – sufficient here for the toe of the Christmas stocking of every child in Ireland. The soft island breeze was heavy with the scent of pines, sea, flowers and tangerines.

In Advent the Sisters received many gifts, including cakes and large baskets of fruit and flowers from their rich ex-patients. The bathroom was full to overflowing with choice blooms. Most of the baskets of dainties were at once distributed to the poor. The nurses received a large share and the two 'misses' were not forgotten. When there was a death in the hospital and the Sisters were asked about an undertaker, they usually recommended 'N', because unlike some of his ilk, he did not over-charge. 'N' remembered the Sisters with gratitude at Xmas and an enormous rum cake was delivered with *'tanti saluti'*. 'N' was not to know that the Sisters did not like rum cake, but 'the misses' did. Day after day in the afternoon, a tea tray was duly deposited in one of our rooms and we tucked into our exquisite snack.

'This will ruin our complexions,' I stated, happily munching.

'And our figures. I wonder if it's finished yet?'

Part of the pleasure was the fact that we never knew for certain whether it would arrive or not.

As the time passed and Christmas day drew nearer, the amount of patients in the *Regina Maris* also dwindled. We therefore had very few patients in the hospital for Christmas. Most of the staff were allowed to go home for a few days. This meant a great deal to the nurses, as nowhere are family ties so strong as in Italy. By Christmas Eve the place had quietened considerably. Cathleen and I, after a last check on our presents, retired to bed for a few hours as we would be attending Midnight Mass with the Sisters at Santa Maria del Parto, a little Church near the hospital which was practically reserved for fishermen and their kin.

We arose at 10 p.m. and dressed in our new frocks which had to be paraded for the nuns' admiration. The dresses were beautifully made and we received the acme of praise when the Sisters stated, 'we were just like Italians'. We had bought native shoes also, which were the height of fashion with their very pointed toes and *extremely* high heels.

'Surely they can't be comfortable?' demanded Mother.

'One has to suffer to be *'elegante'*, Mother,' I replied. They *were* a trifle tight.

We hurried to the Chapel to secure a place, and found that the first three benches had been reserved for the nuns and the Irish Signorinas (whom many people thought were also going to be nuns).

The little Chapel was gaily, if rather flamboyantly, decorated for the Feast. Above the Altar the Madonna, a motherly Neapolitan type of Madonna, looked down benevolently and with a slight smile at her children. She wore jewelled ear-rings which sparkled in the candle light.

Before Mass there was a little procession to the side Altar where the Priest solemnly lifted a white cloth to reveal the figure of The Holy Bambino, rotund and resplendent in a golden nappie!

More lights were lit. The Madonna's jewels sparkled more brightly and she smiled more broadly. She had reason to smile – the congregation had started to sing.

I was always slightly startled at the singing in this Church. One is so accustomed to magnificent Italian voices, that it is rather a shock to discover that *all* Italian voices are by no means magnificent.

The people of this congregation, whether they could sing, or not, expanded their lungs, opened their mouths wide, and uninhibited, let out the sound. The Bambino was welcomed into the world with raucous and joyous bellows of song. Gaily they sang, always a few bars ahead of the organ, a welcome to the Child and compliments to the Mother – *'Della Stella siete piu bella'* – 'You are more beautiful than the stars'.

The Mass, unchanged and solemnly beautiful, was the same as the world over. Here in the warm night of Naples the Priest was offering the same Sacrifice as our Priest and families were offering in Ireland.

When the time came for the Priest's sermon, there was a delightful innovation. After some scuffling among the altar boys a little chap detached himself and with a solemn air, mounted the pulpit. Then, with a wide grin, he addressed the congregation. In beautiful Italian and with many gestures our little orator preached the message of peace and goodwill to a very attentive congregation. This is a lovely custom and the boy preacher is a regular feature of Christmas sermons in the South. After Mass the congregation all trooped by the Altar to kiss the Bambino.

When we returned from Mass, Mother brought us in a huge tray of tea and cakes and our Christmas post. What a collection there was. Our friends and relatives had all remembered that particular section of society referred to as 'exiles'. In their compassion they showered us with perfume, nylons, frilly underwear and all the delicious luxuries one can never afford to buy for oneself.

'Do you know that if I were at home I would have to give away most of these presents to other people for whom I couldn't afford gifts?' asked Cathleen.

'Well this year we'll enjoy our "luxuries",' I replied. 'When we go to Roccarosso I'm looking forward to trying out all this stuff,' I said, sniffing happily at some bottles of high class cosmetics which a rather stern maiden aunt had unexpectedly sent to me. There were two magnificent mantillas which was the Sisters' gift to us. Also I found among my gifts a necklace from Rosario which exactly matched my new dress, and the handbag from Cathleen was one I had always coveted.

We decided to steal in the nuns' present while they were at supper and opening their post. We slipped quietly inside the door of their Department, deposited the gifts, rang loudly on the bell, then flew back to my room. We grinned happily as we heard the yells of excitement and pleasure, emerging from the usually quiet congregation's department. Then our door was flung open and they all entered, all talking at once. 'How did you know I needed slippers?' 'This wool is a perfect shade'. 'I can't wait to get buried in my book'. And from us, 'How do you expect us to pray in Chapel wearing these Mantillas? All I'll do from now on is to pose!' We got as much pleasure from their surprise and delight at their gifts as we did in opening our own. At last Mother called curfew and we were all hustled to bed.

On Christmas morning the nuns rose again for early Mass. The day on duty was rather busy. True we had few patients, but we also had a skeleton staff. The patients, petty at being separated from their beloved *'parente'* on Christmas Day, were inclined to be trying. We were kept occupied answering their bells.

Lunch was a magnificent spread – Crostone in Brodo, Ravioli, Champagne, etc. The gaiety of a festive meal was missing though, as the few girls who couldn't get home for Christmas were nearly in tears.

I was alone on duty in the afternoon. As the patients were sleeping off their dinners, the landing was peaceful. I was glad though when the clock struck five o'clock and Sister

Ann came to relieve me for the evening.

The evening proved a great surprise. The Sisters had invited two Irish women holidaying in Naples, to dinner. We were also invited. It was a real Irish dinner consisting of turkey, ham, stuffing, roast potatoes, peas, plum pudding and wine or champagne to drink. Perhaps it was the champagne which prompted me to give a very lively rendering of 'I Tuoi Baci' – 'Your kisses are like electric shocks' – an Italian rock 'n roll number.

Later we watched Aladdin on television – a very different version from the pantomime hero we remembered. This finger kissing, ravioli eating young man, who attracted the heroine's attention with the sibilant hiss of the Neapolitan, had us highly amused.

When the pantomime was over the Sisters left us for a time to say their prayers. When they returned they joined us in some Christmas cake and wine and we sat around munching and talking of former Christmasses in Ireland. Before the evening ended, Sister Patrick made our day complete by granting us official permission for our trip to Rivisondoli for the winter sports on the second of January. We went to bed well content with our first Neapolitan Christmas.

CHAPTER 14

WINTER SPORTS

On Holy Innocents' Day it was a tradition in the Convent that the youngest nun should rule. The order of seniority was completely reversed and Sister Concepta took the place of Rev. Mother. Sister Margaret became her Assistant. That morning the Sisters came on duty very bleary-eyed. The new Rev. Mother having treated them to apple-pie beds the night before, had called them at four that morning. What is more, breakfast had been a fiasco with milk in the tea-pot, salt in the sugar bowl and so on.

'I'm simply starving,' confided Sister Bernadette to me, as she broke all rules to drink some *latte cafe* behind the kitchen door. 'Goodness knows what other tortures she has planned for us either,' she moaned.

After lunch, when the nuns were all thinking longingly of their beds for a brief siesta after the early call, Sister Concepta announced in firm tones, 'Now Sisters, you will all take a brisk walk in the fresh air and consider what you will do to entertain at the concert which you are giving me tonight.

Sister Margaret and I have to attend to important work.' The two young nuns grinning, saw the others off from the door.

Sister Concepta wasn't grinning when she whistled by me in the corridor half-an-hour later. She was frantic.

Grabbing my arm, she babbled. 'Oh Sheila, hurry. Get Rev. Mother quickly. There is a Bishop in the parlour.'

'You can't keep him waiting then,' I replied cruelly.

'I know, I know,' she said, wringing her hands, 'but I couldn't entertain a Bishop.'

'What about Margaret?'

'Oh, she says she'll carry in any refreshments, but *I* must entertain him. I'll go in then,' she said in her braving-the-lion voice, 'but get Rev. Mother quickly,' she ended on a squeak.

On my way out, my attention was attracted to the balcony of the parlour, where the Sisters were collected in a group, peeping into the room. 'He is no ordinary Bishop,' I thought.

I gave Mother the message.

'Tell her I can't come,' she replied, 'I'm learning a song for tonight.'

When I told Concepta, she looked more terrified than ever. 'Oh dear, oh dear, I wish I were Sister Concepta again. He seems a most difficult Bishop. Of course maybe they are all like that. He says he doesn't like sandwiches, he wants rum babas. Where will I get them?' she wailed.

'They have them at the bar, fifty lira each.'

'Do you think two would do?'

'Better get three, after all he is a Bishop,' Margaret joined in the discussion. 'We should buy four,' she said seriously, 'then he'd feel better if he wanted to eat three, there would be one left on the plate. I *love* rum babas,' she added innocently.

Eventually the purchase was made and I believe His Lordship ate all four before he revealed himself as Sister Joan. A born actress – when she had dressed herself in the parish priest's hat and coat, added a pair of sun glasses and an assumed accent, she would have passed for a Bishop even at the Vatican.

After the fun on Holy Innocents' Day, we all looked forward to New Year's Eve in three days' time.

New Year's Eve was celebrated in Naples with great merry-making. The Sisters had warned us not to go out that evening. 'No one stirs out on New Year's Eve, as it is too dangerous, with all the squibs and fire-crackers. If the girls are not given the day off, they spend the night in the hospital.'

We went up on the flat roof at about eleven. I loved the view from the roof by day, but at night it was particularly entrancing.

Tonight, as we looked into the curtainless windows of the flats surrounding us, we could see the families gathered together feasting and merry-making. People stood at their balconies clutching lighted sparklers, the stars falling in showers on to the streets below. This scene was repeated in a million homes throughout the city, so that Naples was now washed in stars. Just before midnight, the Neapolitans came out on to their balconies and drank toasts to one another. Then the bells from hundreds of Churches pealed out. The peals were accompanied by the crashing of china, as the people, in childish glee, threw every bit of broken china and bottles collected from the previous year, on to the deserted pavements below. The deafening din was supplemented by a fiasco of exploding fireworks which vividly lit the heavens as shooting stars, catherine wheels and fountains painted the sky in an unforgettable display of colours and shapes. Cathleen and I felt as gay as schoolboys as we applauded each successive celestial exhibition. Of course, half the reason for our high spirits was the fact that in two days' time we would be leaving for the mountains.

We had shopped for skiing outfits and we had already done our packing. We were quite ready. Ready that is, except for pocket money. If we were to allow sufficient for our fare and the hotel, we would not have any pocket money – our ski outfits had been dearer than we expected or, more truthfully, we had been carried away by the more dashing fashions, instead of the economy wear. As always, to forget our problems we took a walk. We decided to go to the Evening Mass at San Antonio. This Saint was a great favourite with the Neapolitans and they all attributed many favours and cures to the intercession of the powerful Saint with the Divine Bambino. After all, they assured one another, a Saint who had personal visits from the Lord whom he held as a baby in his arms, must have great influence, and 'influence' was a very important factor in obtaining favours in Neapolitan life.

The little old-fashioned church was packed, and even though we were early we had difficulty in getting in. We quickly discovered that this was another Feast Day of the Saint, who seemed to have far more than his share of birthdays.

The Evening Mass was specially beautiful, for instead of the usual organ and choir, the music was provided by violins.

'San Antonio prega per noi,' chanted the Priest, and the congregation devoutly prayed for cures, jobs, homes, male children and all the 'daily bread' of simple folk. All this while two very unworthy nurses asked the kindly-looking Saint for their pocket money for winter sports.

Within three days we received a letter which contained sufficient to cover our expenses.

It was from two doctor friends who had turned up unexpectedly during the summer: 'Thank you for making our trip to Naples so enjoyable. Buy yourselves a little gift as we don't know what we could send through the customs, Love, Cornflakes and Ginger'. We gazed at one another in awe. 'It worked,' we gasped, a trifle irreverently.

On this journey to Rivisondoli, we were attired warmly in woollens. It would be very cold in the higher altitude. We left a cool but sunny Naples and the air grew colder and colder as our 'bus climbed higher into the mountains. We were lucky enough to have seats on the 'bus, although they were not together. I was seated beside a young man in soldier's uniform. He addressed one or two remarks to me, but not wishing to be drawn into conversation, I pretended not to understand him and turned my head away to look out the window. He did not disturb me further. My unfriendliness could be excused by the fact that both Cathleen and I were thoroughly fed up with strangers in Naples who foisted their attention on us. They would walk in step with us and although completely ignored, persisted, 'You like company?' sometimes even having the audacity to link us. With a three hour 'bus journey ahead of me therefore, I did not risk encouraging even light conversation with my neighbour. He in his turn, sat quietly (with an expression of the most abject misery on his face) staring into space, lost in his own thoughts.

As the snaking road climbed higher into the pine clad mountains, our breath made little clouds as it hit the cold air. I felt chilly and turned to close the window. 'Allow me,' said my seat companion and he closed it for me. With a pleasant smile he again subsided into his seat and was soon lost again in thought, with an expression of acute loneliness on his face.

'Poor fellow,' I thought, 'he looks miserable. I wonder what is wrong? Maybe I was rude not to speak to him.' I turned to him and said, 'Thank you for closing the window. It is cold here, isn't it?'

His face suffused with pleasure when I spoke. 'You know Italian?' He then told me he was a Calabrian living in the extreme toe of Italy. He was now doing his year of National Service in the army, a year compulsory for all. Mario, as he introduced himself, had been at home for Christmas and was now returning to camp. 'I have six more months to go before I am free. How I hate the army!' he added vehemently.

'Why do you hate it so?'

'Because it has taken me away from my home in beautiful Calabria – away from my father. I have to wear this terrible uniform and share a room with peasants.' Though Mario was an educated and cultured man, this was the first time he had left home.

'But surely,' I argued, 'you want to travel – to see other countries, other peoples, or at least to know your *own* country.'

'No,' he pouted, 'I don't. I only want to know and love Calabria, where I could be happy for the rest of my life. My father came as far as Naples with me. When he left I had tears in my eyes.'

'That was not very brave of you. You might have spared a thought for your father's feelings.'

'I could not help it,' he stated simply, 'it was stronger than I.' I did not smile at the melodramatic statement. I could understand perfectly how the pain of a family separation was all the more terrible when it had been delayed until the manhood of a boy, whose hopes were pinned no further than his home and county.

'This is a time on which I shall always look back with horror as the saddest time in my life. I will never leave Calabria again after this,' he told me. His boyish vehemence made me feel much older than he, though we were of the same age.

'Try not to look on the army training just as a period to be endured,' I consoled. 'It is an opportunity to see more of your country and meet more of its people. This separation from your people will also make you realize the suffering of families during war, so that you will become another voice in the demand for peace.'

A little boy detached himself from his mother and toddled inquisitively the length of the 'bus. Then with the instinct of a young animal, he selected the soldier and leaned confidently against his knees. Mario, without interrupting the conversation, put a protecting arm around him and made the little head comfortable against his side. He openly and unselfconsciously showed a charming tenderness towards the child – a trait of character strong in the Italian people. He told me a little about his family.

'My mother died when I was twelve. She was a wonderful musician and used to teach me the piano. See, here is her photograph and this is Padre and this is one of me. Do you wish to have it?' I accepted the photograph.

As the 'bus toiled and laboured over the ice-slippery roads, we talked. He described his home, his way of life, his friends, his love of music, building with each sentence a picture of the man. I in my turn, told of our way of life and explained as best I could that my curiosity about another country did *not* mean I did not care for my own.

'When I lived in Ireland I never loved her

as much as I do now,' I explained sincerely.

He would interrupt from time to time to point out the window at some unexpectedly beautiful sight.

'Look Sheila, how the evening sun lights that little cloud,' or 'See the splendid water-fall.'

Sometimes as I spoke, a smile would play around the corners of his mouth.

'What is it, Mario? Why do you smile?'

'It is your accent, so *sympatica*. You know, I have never met a girl who talks as you do. Seriously, a girl has never spoken like you before.'

That was quite possible. A Calabrian girl would never criticize or offer advice to a man. They also had the additional handicap of the chaperone as a deterrent to free speech whenever in the company of a member of the opposite sex. Added to this, a young man introduced into the home of a Calabrian girl was usually looked upon solely as a possible husband. One could not blame the girls for even speechlessness!

He showed me the six stars on his watch strap, one for each month of service completed, and he amused me with anecdotes about army life. My companion could be quite entertaining when he forgot his woes. I could not believe we were already at Roccarasso when Cathleen suddenly attracted my attention.

'Sheila, we are here. The signpost says Roccarasso, though it looks different with the snow.'

I said goodbye to Mario and we scrambled off the 'bus. Our fellow travellers called 'Enjoy yourselves', and waved as the 'bus drew out of sight.

This time when we descended from the 'bus, there were no waiting nuns to greet us. We stepped out of the warmth and were met by a blast of icy wind which bit like needles into our skin. Carrying our cases, we commenced the three mile walk to Rivisondoli. How had it seemed so short in summer? How tired and hungry, our light cases getting heavier at every step, we struggled along the interminable road in cold which brought water to our eyes.

'What on earth will we do,' Cathleen wailed, 'if they haven't room for us?' We had rushed off enthusiastically, without pausing to book a hotel room. 'I suppose we would have to walk all the way back to Roccarasso and try for a hotel there,' she mused aloud.

'No fear,' I rejoined, 'I'm blowed if I will cover this ground again tonight. I'll sit on their doorstep and bawl, and even if they put me in with the cow, I'd prefer it to suffering this cold any longer. Anyway, I always wanted to sleep a night in a hay barn, did you, Cathleen?'

'No, there would be mice,' she answered,

practical as ever. 'Our letter of introduction from the Sisters should be a great help,' she reminded me consolingly.

The hotel was full when we arrived, but our letter from the Sisters was the 'open Sesame' to every hospitality. The proprietor of the hotel found us a night's lodging in a nearby house and the following morning we moved to the hotel. Fortunately for both of us, we had neither to sleep in a barn or walk another three miles. Our bedroom with private bathroom, boasted one large bed. After I became used to Cathleen's incessant conversation while asleep and she grew accustomed to my 'salmon-jumps', we both slept soundly together.

Next morning, attired in ski pants and warm, colourful jackets, we novices to winter sports ate hot, buttered rolls and drank plenty of scalding coffee to insulate us from the biting cold. We were pleasantly surprised when we did go out, as we did not feel cold. The bright sunshine shone strongly, warming us and making the snow-covered countryside glisten as though scattered with Christmas tinsel. Against the white mantle of snow, the enamel green pine trees made a vivid contrast, while on every slope skiers and would-be skiers in their bright jerseys looked very gay.

We took a long walk, thrilled at the exciting difference the winter had made in our beloved valley.

At lunch we were ready for the many courses of delicious food put before us. After lunch we were lazily planning a siesta when we were hailed by two boys we had met formerly as relatives of Doctor Grimaldi. They greeted us as long-lost sisters. Scorning our plan for a siesta, they informed us that they were taking us 'to play'.

The sparkling clear air, sunshine and snow soon made us feel rejuvenated and we were ready 'to play'. We called our two friends 'Red' and 'Black' after the shades of their pullovers. Called after ancient Roman generals, their real names were too difficult to remember. After a long walk we reached an unoccupied slope. Very quickly we made the discovery that there was more to skiing than just buckling on one's skis and taking off to glide like a bird down the slippery slopes. I *did* glide down the slopes alright, frequently, but it was on my 'bottom' rather than my skis. Red jersey suggested that I try a toboggan – this was better. I sat on the little toboggan and went hurtling down the slopes, yelling in mingled fear and excitement, a menace to anyone in my way. With laudable fortitude, Red jersey hauled my toboggan back to the top of the hill after each ride. Cathleen meanwhile, with commendable determination, was receiving a skiing lesson from Black jersey. She looked like a cuddlesome baby bear as she took tumble after tumble in the powdery snow. Time passed quickly in our enjoyment, until the sun began to set and we all decided to get back quickly before the bitter cold which fell after sunset. Cathleen and I were thrilled to discover we hadn't to attempt the long walk back – the boys had ordered a horse-drawn sleigh. There it stood, the horses stamping impatiently and jingling their harness, the yellow-toothed driver cracking his whip. Wrapped in rugs, we rode silently and smoothly over the snowy fields.

The boys sang folk-songs and a little ditty composed by Red jersey of which he was inordinately proud. My companions' faces glowed with colour from the cold and the exciting exercise. The smell of the horse and the pines mingled pleasantly and the air tasted of iced beer. It was the ideal way to finish the day's sport – this journey in a winter wonderland – while the sinking sun wounded the evening sky.

Back at the hotel we hurried to bath and change for dinner. The evening before we had changed into dresses for dinner, expecting this to be the usual thing at the premier hotel of a winter sports resort. To our consternation, on arriving at the dining room, we appeared to be the only people to have done so. 'For heaven's sake act as if this were the most usual thing in the world,' I hissed to Cathleen, who looked ready to bolt. She straightened her back and proceeded with me to the table where we were soon, assisted by the head waiter, choosing our menu and apparently unconcerned at the stares we were receiving. Two very attractive men, whose skill on their skis Cathleen and I had admired earlier, stopped at our table, exchanged a few pleasantries and complimented us on our beauty, before seating themselves at a nearby table, where they gazed on us with an expression of exaggerated admiration.

'Don't worry Kate,' I told her. 'We are dressed correctly and all these other people are not.' I was far from convinced by my own words, but I didn't want her to feel as uncomfortable as I at the glances we were receiving.

'You sound like the woman who said all the soldiers were out of step except her Johnny,' Cathleen laughed, but we began to relax and enjoy the lovely dinner and after a glass of the sparkling native wine, we could even smile at the burning gazes of the men at the next table.

This evening we were not the only ones 'dressed' for dinner. Some of the other women had changed into becoming dresses.

After dinner all the guests usually drifted to the great lounge, the focal point of which was the enormous log fire. It took two men to carry the weight of the great blocks of timber which this magnificent fire devoured. The guests divided themselves into graceful little groups to discuss the day's sport, watch television or just to relax around the fire and watch the leaping flames.

Black and Red jersey came over to us.

'You'll both have every mother in the place at your throats if you don't behave yourselves.'

'What on earth for?' we indignantly questioned.

'Don't try to tell us you weren't making eyes at your neighbours at the next table,' they declared.

'They were doing the staring,' Cathleen defied.

'You weren't too adverse to them, judging by the smiles you were flashing on and off like beacons. Why for one of those smiles I'd go through fire and brimstone,' declared our prosecutor.

'I don't see where all this is leading,' Cathleen stated flatly. 'Who are the two glamour boys anyway?' she asked.

Black and Red looked at one another, surprised.

'You don't know?' Red explained. 'The tall hawk-faced one is the Baron Aureuleus – a very wealthy landowner, with him is his equally rich cousin Count Alexander.'

'I believe he bought his title,' interrupted

Black cattily.

'They are both very eligible bachelors,' continued Red, 'hence the stir among the Mothers and maidens when they came in a few minutes ago.'

'They are here now.'

'Yes, at the bar. You two seem to be the only pair in the room who don't get into a flutter when they come in.'

Now that the fact had been pointed out to us, we did notice quite a fuss being made of these two. We were aware that many of the parents present, with grown-up daughters, had hoped to find such eligible bachelors among the guests.

Cathleen and I began to enjoy the pantomime, as the poor fellows were pounced on by eager mothers, whose daughters meanwhile, posed becomingly in the latest 'après ski' creations of the best couturiers.

'They really are heavenly creatures, these Italian girls,' I sighed a little enviously, as I watched a dainty creature in green corduroy, whose jet black hair and huge, dark eyes were an electric contrast to her flawless white skin. 'You don't look too bad yourself,' Cathleen assured me with a grin. I smiled back and we took out our books and began to read.

Soon, immersed in a world of crinolines, straw bonnets, carriages and pairs and stately mansions, I felt a shadow fall across my page.

It was the Baron Aureuleus – 'wealthy landowner' and 'most eligible of bachelors'.

Human nature being what it is, he was only interested in the only persons in the room who had not even noticed his presence at the hotel. Some devil made me smile a gracious welcome. The same devil must have been at work on Cathleen. The Count was seated by her side in earnest conversation while she listened in apparent grave wonder.

After much beating about the bush, disguised as an exchange of compliments and learned discussions on everything from ceramics to ancient Irish folklore, our admirers asked if we would 'Come to visit the ski club at Roccarasso?'

We were delighted to have a change of occupation from the endless fire-worship each evening at the hotel. Our respective devils too, noted with gratification, the envious eyes of the other ladies present as we left the lounge. Cathleen, noticing their envy, said to me as we prepared to go out.

'They needn't be envious, they are only a pair of stuffed shirts.'

'Come on Countess,' I said, 'We'll teach them to enjoy themselves.'

'You would make a super Baroness,' she giggled, as the lift carried us down to our titled escorts.

At the ski club our escorts, who were

187

inclined to be very formal and superior, relaxed a little. Soon they were introduced by us to the intricacies of Irish Ceilidh dancing. They took to it like ducks to water and before long were giving quite a creditable performance, to the delight of the younger set at the club. Not being used to Irish dancing, they were soon out of breath. While they recovered, we deserted them shamefully for another group who were anxious to learn our National dances. That evening, probably for the first time in history, the walls of the Roccorasso ski club shook to the 'Walls of Limerick', the 'Haymakers' Jig' and as a grand finale Cathleen led the Count, and I the Baron, in the gay 'Waves of Tory'.

The following morning we met our two noble friends hobbling painfully into the dining room.

'Every muscle in my body is on fire after your dances,' moaned the Count.

'Skiing was never as painful,' sighed the Baron, ruefully.

Though we were not particularly sad, we expressed our regret politely when urgent business recalled the two noblemen from their holiday. Happily we went back 'to play' with the two faithfuls, Red Jersey and Black Jersey, who were more fun than our rather bumptious, proud and over dignified previous escorts.

CHAPTER 15

EPIPHANY

Despite the gaiety of the winter sports, people looked forward most to the representation of the crib. Everywhere one could hear speculation as to the identity of the Madonna this year. Not only must the girl be young and beautiful and a native of the province, but she must also be virtuous. It was a great honour to play the part of the Virgin.

St. Joseph would be played by the village postmaster – with his air of venerable dignity and his beard: there would be little difficulty about make-up.

The central figure of the infant Jesus would be the six-week-old bouncing baby son of Francesca and Giovanni Galassi. Being the youngest baby in the village, his right to the role was unchallenged.

Except for the part of the three wise kings from the East, everyone else of the one thousand villagers played the role of their everyday lives. Roles of innkeepers, craftsmen, peasants and shepherds. There would be no technical direction, but merely a coordination of actions. Everyone wondered how this representation would turn out, as they wandered around the snow-clad village examining the preparations. The army were busy floodlighting for the occasion and the soldiers wandered around, glad of a respite from their usual routine.

A small cave-like dwelling representing the stable of Bethlehem had been built in a large, flat field at the foot of the village, in front of which the spectators would watch the action.

After dinner that evening, everyone muffled up in several thicknesses of clothing and set out for the scene of action. In spite of our jerseys and fur-lined coats, Cathleen and I shivered in the biting cold. The moment the sun sank Rivisondoli was bitterly cold. At the gate, we showed our tickets and were directed to a place on a makeshift grandstand erected for the occasion. Though we were early, I was amazed at the huge crowd already gathered there. 'Bus loads of people kept arriving to swell the throng – Americans, English, German, French, but mostly Italians. For the Italians this was a yearly affair – one could see that by the way they had come prepared with furs and blankets and flasks of hot coffee to guard themselves from the cold.

The village was in darkness and the only light was the cold glitter of stars and snow.

Suddenly a spotlight high in the village picked out the figure of Caesar Augustus on his throne. Then the gleam of bannered trumpets raised by Roman soldiers was seen and a man's skilfully amplified voice, which seemed to come from every point of the village and surrounding hills, spoke the narrative in the bare words of the gospel: –

'There went out a decree from Caesar Augustus that the whole world should be enrolled.'

The trumpeters, to whom all eyes were drawn instinctively, raised their trumpets to their lips and blew a fanfare to the four corners of the world to proclaim the great Caesar's order.

The spotlight now picked up two lonely figures, a man and a woman, travelling along the road. The man led a little donkey, on which sat the young woman, a weary droop to her shoulders.

The narrator continued:

'And Joseph also went up from Galilee out of the city of Nazareth into Judea, to the city of David, which is called Bethlehem: because he was of the house and family of David, to be enrolled with Mary his espoused wife...'

We watched as Joseph and Mary knocked wearily on two innkeepers' doors and were turned away. At the third door we could see the innkeeper shake his head – he had no room. Joseph appeared to be pleading – Mary was with child, her time was up. Finally the innkeeper pointed to the field below, indicating the stable. The couple journeyed towards the stable which was also in darkness.

In the meantime the spotlight showed the shepherds on the hillsides watching their flocks, and we heard the angelic message they received.

'...Fear not ... for this day is born to you a Saviour.' We heard the crowing of a cock, the startled neigh of a horse, the lowing of a cow and then a medley of animal voices, as the creatures of the world paid homage. The bells of the village rang out and the whole village sprang to life as the houses, including the cave, were flooded in light.

In the cave, Mary and Joseph knelt in adoration of the baby, wrapped in swaddling clothes and laid in a manger. Behind them the breath of an ox and an ass clouded the cold air.

The baby awoke and began to cry. Mary rocked Him and the infant slept again. Down through the cobbled streets of the ancient village ran the excited shepherds, shouting the good news as... 'they came with haste: and they found Mary and the infant lying in the manger'. Bowing down, the shepherds adored the child, offering him gifts of new-born lambs, which they were carrying slung over their shoulders.

Then we heard the strange, plaintive sounds of oriental music and the three wise kings of the East appeared, their servants bowed down with the weight of costly gifts.

'...and behold the star which they had seen in the East went before them, until it came and stood over where the child was...' The three kings adored the child and offered their gifts; gold, frankincense and myrrh.

Now came the most wonderful sight. The big news had spread through the country-side and everyone wished to see the wonder for himself. From the nearby mountains and from every street in the village we saw the laughing, skipping, running people dressed in the marvellously gay costumes of Abruzzi. No one was empty-handed, and when they had genuflected in adoration of the baby, they laid their gifts at the opening of the stable – gifts of newly baked bread, live hens, cheese, baskets of eggs, fruit and vegetables. All of them carried torches which they lit at the stable. The vivid hues of the magnificent traditional costumes leapt to glowing life under the orange glow of their flaming torches. A choir singing softly high in the village began the Christmas hymn – *Tu 'scendi dalle Stelle* – 'You came down from the stars, Oh king of the heavens'.

The adorers at the manger joined in the

song to their 'divine bambino'.

In the glorious moments of the grand finale, the clock was put back over a thousand years, as everyone present, including bystanders, joined in the chorus. The crescendo of music echoed and re-echoed in the manger, the village and the hills, until the whole valley was a bowl of joyous song.

Still under the spell of what they had seen, the crowds dispersed, silently, to their homes, their hearts filled with the angelic benediction of peace and goodwill.

Our feelings of peace and goodwill lasted for approximately five minutes, then, rounding a corner, we ran into a snowball ambush, prepared by Red Jersey and Black Jersey. We retaliated promptly. Our ranks were swelled by the by-passers, who became involved. Finally there were at least half-a-hundred warriors, shouting their war cries and pelting one another with snow. The battle raged fiercely until, in the final stages, one ceased to bother about who was 'friend' or 'enemy' and we just pasted one another *ad lib*. Finally, weakened by laughter, the troops called a halt to the campaign and we returned to our hotel, having made more friends in the fifteen minutes 'battle' than the whole of the preceding week.

The remaining days of our 'Winter Sports' holiday passed quickly. The bright January sunshine reflected from the snow had given us a quite creditable suntan. We had played in the snow all day, slept like babies at night and eaten meals which would have done credit to a farmer.

Aglow with health and vitality, we took the return 'bus to Naples.

'I feel I could handle the most cussed patient,' declared Cathleen.

'If Mephistopheles himself were admitted with an acute appendix, I'd pamper him, I'm feeling so full of goodwill,' I agreed with her. Our first winter holiday had been an unqualified success.

At the hospital the Sisters had prepared for our return – our bedrooms had been spring-cleaned and vases of roses filled the air with perfume. Supper was prepared for us in the Sisters' parlour. Here they gathered to welcome us home and exchange news. The Sisters' most important piece of news was that the youngest members of the community, Margaret and Concepta, had been finally received into the order. The two new brides – Margaret, with her usual *joie de vivre*, Concepta, a trifle shyer – came forward to proudly show their rings. Their happiness was obvious and was reflected in the faces around them. I was glad of the native custom which allowed us to kiss their hands.

CHAPTER 16

BUONA SERA SIGNORINA

One particularly busy week in which patients streamed into the hospital in an unending flow, we had several bad accident cases and the surgeons appeared to be putting in overtime. Added to all this we had the builders in the hospital. The place seemed to be covered in dust and tools, and the incessant noise was trying, for both patients and staff.

Though the hospital was a very new building, a huge crack had appeared on the roof of the Men's Ward. A surveyor was called, who decided the roof needed to be stripped and reinforced. Our patients were evacuated and I had my first experience of the Italian workman.

Twenty young men in dungarees and wearing paper hats to protect their hair, were hard at work when we arrived on duty. They eyed every nurse who passed from head to foot and if the foreman was not about, called *'Bella, Bella'*, or twisted their fingers on their cheeks in a sign of approval. Apart from these distractions, they seemed to work very hard. At eleven o'clock one of the workmen, a diminutive chap, appeared at the kitchen door – billycan in hand.

'Tea?' I asked.

'No Signorina, could I disturb you to let me heat the coffee,' he replied courteously.

On questioning him, I discovered he was only nine years of age. He told me he had been working a year now and was very proud to be earning his food in exchange for any help he could give.

When I questioned the Sisters about this exploitation of mere babies, Sister Patrick explained that the small fellow was far better off than many children in Naples, 'at least his belly is full'.

At lunch time the men all ceased work. From brown-paper parcels they produced huge long loaves, split lengthwise and filled with cheese, tomatoes, egg or spinach. (They would set to with a will and consume these huge loaves of bread). Many of them swapped half a loaf with a fellow worker, breaking it with his hands, and he thus had two varieties of fillings for his repast. They each contributed a lump of their food for the youngest member. Then, seating themselves on the floor with their backs to the wall, they would nod and smile at one another wishing each other *'Buon appetito'* – 'good appetite'.

After the meal, they stretched out on the hard floor and slept soundly for the period of the siesta. They then went back to work again until evening. At the end of the day they all washed, changed out of their working clothes, and left the building carrying their working clothes in smart brief cases and looking like white-collar workers.

At the end of three weeks the repairs were completed. We nurses made up the ward beds, while the builders, all spruced and shining, complete with brief cases, stood outside the door awaiting the ceremonial opening by Professor Caracciolo, when we would all receive coffee and sweet cakes. The Professor arrived with his assistants. His rubicund face beaming, he shook hands with the foreman and they exchanged compliments. Just as Caracciolo prepared to step into the room there was an ominous rumble as of thunder and the room and corridor were enveloped in a cloud of dust, as the roof caved in. We all scattered in every direction. As the dust settled, everyone had a remark to pass about the catastrophe.

'Thank God we had not admitted patients,' said the nuns. 'Three more weeks steady work,' said the labourers. 'Let's eat the cakes while they are distracted,' said the nurses. 'It was the climate. We had too much sun,' said the foreman.

'Tell administration that the cost of all de-luxe rooms is to be raised 500 lira per day,' said the Professor, and with a philosophic shrug he continued his ward rounds.

I was busily engaged dispensing the morning medicines later, when Sister Patrick called me.

'There is a visitor downstairs for you, Sheila.'

I couldn't leave my work undone, so I finished giving the medicines. Professor Morelli was in one of the rooms when I entered, 'I wish to do this dressing, will you assist me please?' By the time I was finished, my visitor had been waiting an hour. I excused myself to Sister and ran downstairs to find Neill O'Connor patiently waiting in the parlour. He was in Naples for one more visit before his unit would be transferred to California. He stood up with a smile, but I, suddenly realizing that my hair needed washing and that my uniform was blood-stained, thought 'Why on earth didn't he warn me he was coming?' and instead of a word of welcome, I said crossly, 'What the *blazes* are you doing here?' Then, relenting a little at his stricken face, I temporised, 'I've already had my off-duty for this week. Had I known you were coming I would have saved it.'

His face cleared. 'Never mind, Sister Francis will see that you get off-duty to see me. She is a great woman,' he added enthusiastically. I refrained from saying that Sister Francis had nothing to do with the nursing side of the hospital. Hers was the responsibility of catering and laundry.

'I'll meet you at ten past five, but now I must hurry back to the ward,' I promised and left him. On duty that afternoon I was unable to keep the smile of pleased anticipation from my lips.

'Look at her,' said Sister Bernadette, 'She is like a cat after cream. Where are you going tonight?'

'I don't know. I'll ask Sister Francis's advice. She is an authority on night clubs.'

'What time is he calling for you?'

'Ten past five. That gives me ten minutes to prepare.'

'I'm not having this outing spoiled because you won't take time to present yourself well. You are going off duty at four today.'

'You angel,' I exclaimed.

'Less of your *'plamas'* now, off you go with Professor Lorenzotti, *that* will make you earn your off-duty.'

My round with the rather crotchety Lorenzotti went beautifully. The Italian doctors never had the heart to be cross with a smiling nurse! After the round, I volunteered to help Rosario check the linen. We worked very happily together. When making beds or doing treatments, our conversation was restricted and directed towards the patient. When sorting the linen it was a different matter and we could exchange gossip or she would give me the words of the latest *canzone*. 'Would you like to learn *"Tintarella di luna"*?' she asked, stopping work with a bunch of pillowslips in her arms. 'It goes like this,' and she broke into a rock 'n roll tune about two cats.

'Sh-sh-sh – be quiet,' I admonished. 'I'm getting off early today and I don't want to make anyone cross by kicking up a racket.' Then I proceeded to tell her about my date for tonight.

'Is he the tall, fair one who was here last month?'

'Si.'

'Brutto ma sympatico' – (Ugly but nice), declared Rosario and she proceeded to instruct me on how I could look my most glamorous. 'Can I lend you anything – my beads? This flower?'

'No thanks, cara. It is my hair that bothers me. I should have shampooed it yesterday.'

'Never mind, I have just the thing for you,' she answered, going to her handbag and producing a little packet of perfumed powder. 'Shake this on the hair, brush hard and *ecco* – you have shining, clean hair.'

I accepted the packet gratefully and 'Don't forget to lie on your bed with the eyes closed for fifteen minutes – for bright eyes,' warned the little sorceress.

I was very pleased with the result of Rosario's dry shampoo and though I hadn't lain on the bed for the prescribed fifteen minutes, my eyes were bright enough. The very fact of 'dressing up' was enough to give them sparkle. Cathleen and I usually took pains *not* to appear attractive when we took our evening stroll. This involved flat shoes, drab headsquares and no cosmetics. We had even, at times, to wear sour faces, all this to prevent unwelcome company being forced upon us. It was a joy to wear high heels, a very feminine dress, and apply perfume and lipstick, also to know that there would be two opportunities to discard drabness, as Neill was here for two days this time.

I twirled and pirouetted for Sister Francis, who always seemed to be around to see us off. In answer to my query, she suggested we dine at Zi Theresa's at Santa Lucia. This was a welcome suggestion, as both Neill and I had always wished to visit Santa Lucia, made famous by the song.

We ate octopus under the shadow of the Castel d'Uova, listened to the music of mandolins and watched the fishing boats, their lights like twinkling fireflies skimming the bay. Then discovering a mutual love for Anglo-Irish poetry, we recited our favourites as we sauntered home along the selvedge of the bay. From our Irish poetry, we two exiles smiled reminiscently at 'little rabbits in a field at evening, lit by the slanting sun' or sighed over 'pools among the rushes that scarce could bathe a star'. We chuckled over 'Slattery's mounted foot' and felt national pride in 'Stand ye now for Erin's glory'. It was clear that for two of Ireland's children, absence had definitely served to make 'the heart grow fonder'.

Happily, Neill's visit coincided with that of Michael, an old Dublin friend of Cathleen's, who was now working in the Irish Embassy at Rome, so that when we set out next evening, we were a foursome.

The evening began with a motor-boat tour of the bay. How cool and refreshing it was after the heat of the day! Then we took a horse-drawn carriage to Santa Monte for dinner at an open-air restaurant, high above the twinkling lights of Naples and overlooking the beloved bay.

The evening was perfect. Everything and everyone conspired to make our party a success, from the waiters, who were all 'characters' to the band, who fell in love with our party and, deserting their other customers, joined our table for the night. It was one of those rare evenings in which one is absolutely happy and, rarer still, conscious of the fact. The food was delicious, the wine ambrosial and the conversation scintillating. We all felt young, very gay, very alive and ridiculously happy. We danced whirling waltzes and uninhibited tangos with exotic twists, turns and backbends. We ate fresh lobster, drank sparkling Spumante, sang and talked. When two flower-sellers came to our table, the whole contents of their baskets were bought for us. For one night we were Kings and Queens. Finally it was time to go, but the band and waiters, reluctant to leave such *sympatica* folk, followed us down the street to our carozza, singing and playing '*Buona Sera Signorina*'.

Clasping our armloads of flowers, we slowly climbed the marble staircase, until at the top step we sat down together I gazed dreamily out at the star-filled sky. I felt a deep, warm kinship with the rest of humanity. 'How infinite the heavens, how finite are we'. My brain, liberated by the beauty of the night, the glow of the evening and the effect of Spumante, chased after a kaleidescope of whirling thoughts. When I tried to express my lofty thoughts to Cathleen, she eyed me carefully for a moment, then with rapid diagnosis stated flatly, 'Too much Spumante – we'd better go to bed.'

CHAPTER 17

ARRIVEDERCI

My enjoyable outing with the Irishman made me realize how much I was beginning to miss my own country and its people. Though I had lost my heart to the Italians, I still regarded them with the tolerant affection one affords to children. Though the Irish might not be as demonstrative or as complimentary, I still longed for the people who thought, felt and acted as I. Yet, had I been gaining experience in my profession, I might have had some reason to remain on longer. I began to see the flaws in my present placid existence. The life we led practically cut us off completely from the stimulation of English books, theatre, films and, above all, conversation. After much thought I reluctantly decided that I would leave in May, before the intense heat of the summer.

Though the Sisters had hoped I would stay for a two-year term, instead of only eighteen months, they were very understanding.

Before leaving, Cathleen and I hoped to have one more holiday together. We wished to visit, Rome, Assisi and Florence. To our joy we were granted a fortnight's leave. We were given the addresses of suitable hostels at the three places. Gaily we set out and explored other parts of this sunny land.

On our return, the welcome we received back at the *Regina Maris* was as warm as ever. The nuns recounted their adventures of the past fortnight while we eagerly described our holiday. We told them about all the people we had met and the wonders we had seen. Cathleen described her great night at the open-air opera at Rome, and I tried to find words to express my feelings about Assisi. Sister Teresa smiled at my enthusiasm.

'How are you going to leave it at all, Sheila?'

How was I going to leave this land of the sun? It was a question I was to ask myself frequently in the next two months, before my return to the 'Green Isle'.

Next morning we were all agreeably surprised when Pia announced at breakfast that she was engaged to be married. As, contrary to common practice, she had never spoken of a *'fidanzata'*, her news was quite a bombshell. After the preliminary wishes for her happiness had been expressed, the nurses wanted to know who the lucky one was and why she had kept it a secret so long. Pia explained that as she had not a beautiful appearance she feared being jilted and if everyone knew, she would 'cut an ugly figure'. Now she was an engaged woman, her position had altered, the flood gates of silence were opened and a torrent of words flowed out. Her Adriano was everything that was good, strong and kind. He worked on the *funiculare* and was a very important person. He was a cousin of the woman in the flat above hers and they had met many times when she went to baby-sit for the woman. They had gone on the church outing to Monte Faito together and shared their food and wine. It was there that Adriano had proposed. She sighed dramatically and assured us it was a very romantic occasion.

After Pia's dramatic announcement, there followed a rash of love affairs at the hospital. Lucia announced her engagement to the faithful Johnny and Dr. Treves became engaged.

He arrived for his rounds one morning.

'Do you wish to dress the fistula first Doctor Treves?' Carla asked as she wheeled out the dressing trolley.

'*Professor Treves*, if you please,' he replied with mock disgust. Within a few moments he was surrounded by a large group of nurses and *parente*, who clapped his back, shook his hand and even embraced him. Everyone was pleased that his hard work had been crowned with success, and that he had been granted a professorship.

The next time we saw Tina there was a definite change in the girl. She looked radiant, had changed her hair-do and sported a brand new engagement ring. Cathleen and I were enthusiastic that this love affair, in which we had taken a proprietary interest had reached such a satisfactory conclusion.

When I had congratulated Treves on his beautiful and charming bride, I hurried to catch up with my duties as we were a little behind in our chores owing to the houseman's announcement. As I hurried about, changing dressings and taking four-hourly temperatures, I noticed that Rosario and Anna seemed to be missing from the field of battle. I went in search of them and found them (as I expected) giggling in the utility room. Rosario was laughing heartily at something Anna had told her.

'What's the joke?' I asked.

'I've just been in to No. 12,' Anna explained, 'to ask had he answered nature's call or not, but when I entered the room, he was surrounded by so many *parente* and grand folk that I felt a bit shy, you understand? I felt it would be an indelicate question – you understand? I excused myself and withdrew discreetly,' she said with dignity. 'As I was leaving the room I noticed that he was propped up rather high in the bed. *Madre Mia* if he wasn't perched on the throne!' and she collapsed again into giggles.

I tried to maintain some semblance of dignity as I told them to hurry with the work and answer some of the bells which had begun to peal like a new year's eve celebration.

'First come into the utility room, Sheila. I want to show you something,' begged Rosario, her eyes sparkling as she brandished a letter.

Oh dear, I thought, another love letter. I wonder who it can be this time. 'I'll come later, when we have more free time,' I promised.

When I had a spare moment I came. This letter was not from a boy friend, the address was that of a famous school of nursing. I read on. It was a letter accepting the entry of one Rosario as a pupil for general nurse training. It went on to outline the rules and regulations for students – but I read no further. I hugged Rosario while she laughed with pleasure.

'It has always been my plan to become a fully qualified nurse,' she confided.

It was a splendid plan and one of which I thoroughly approved. With her intelligence and natural aptitude I felt she would make a fine nurse. She babbled on delightedly about her new training school. She was to share a room at the hospital with a 'dear friend' who had been to the same convent school as she. Altogether the arrangements seemed ideal. I congratulated her.

'Thank you, Sheila,' she kissed me exuberantly, 'I knew you would be pleased, and that's not all – Bruno is house doctor there.'

'Who on earth is Bruno?' I asked curiously.

'Do you not remember?' She drew out the unfaithful Michele's locket from inside her uniform and snapped it open, revealing a handsome young man. It took me a moment to recognize Doctor Bruno Pero, who had been operated upon for a squint in the summer.

'We have been seeing one another since he left the *Regina Maris*,' she confided, 'and we are getting engaged as soon as he has done his year as a houseman. If I study nursing I will be a great help to Bruno in his career.' Rosario seemed to have done a little serious thinking for a change – her plan to train as a qualified nurse was a good one, and all her friends and relatives approved of her present choice of boy-friend.

As I watched Rosario skip gaily off to answer a bell, all her old gaiety now returned a hundred-fold, I consoled myself with the knowledge that though I was leaving soon, I knew that many of my friends were happier

210

than when I had arrived. 'Besides,' I told myself, 'the place won't be the same without Rosario, Pia and Lucia.'

In these days before leaving, I remembered vividly my earlier experiences. How I had changed! I recalled the time when I thought 'if only I had the courage to answer the telephone everything would be all right'. Now I answered the 'phone without hesitation, and shared in all the chatter and gossip of a large hospital. I remembered how I criticized the Italian women for their complete dependence on their menfolk. 'I don't wear lipstick' one would say, 'because Enso does not like make-up' or 'I can't go to the party, because Papa wants me to finish a pullover which I'm knitting for his feast day'. It took me a long time to discover that the Italian women enjoyed their dependence on their menfolk, and even longer to decide that they were right. They loved, honoured and obeyed the stronger sex and in return were cherished and cared for as all women wish to be. When I discussed my conclusions with Cathleen I said, 'I really believe that they are better off and happier in their dependence than we are with our careers and talk of equal rights. They train seriously for the most worthwhile career for women.'

'Oh no, Sheila,' Cathleen disagreed, 'I should say they are treated often as though they were children.'

I stuck to my guns. 'You are wrong, Cathleen, they only appear to give in all the time to the men. Just like our own women, they capitulate about small issues, but get their way in the important ones and are yet so subtle that the men think that it was their idea in the first place. As for status – who is more important in Italian life than the Mother?'

Finally we did agree that the Italian way of life had much to be said for it. We particularly admired the strong ties which bound their families into one unassailable unit. Certainly in Ireland, family ties are strong, but in Italy the family fortress included uncles, aunts and in-laws with an assortment of cousins to the hundredth degree.

'It only we could retain our own good qualities (if any) and imitate theirs,' sighed Cathleen.

'Yes,' I agreed, 'I wish I could cook, sew and *particularly* dress, like they do.'

'What about their freedom of expression?'

'That is something I admire. I feel we are too inhibited: we conceal our feelings, good or bad. I am not suggesting that we should dispense with self-control and throw tantrums when in a rage, but surely it should not be so difficult for us to express pleasure or affection.'

'I suppose what we'll end up by doing,'

Cathleen added, 'is retaining our Irish vices added to which, when we are crossed, we'll lie down on the floor kicking and screaming!'

My memories of the year and a half, like slides in a lantern show, ranged from the sublime to the ridiculous. I saw the stark Faraglioni rocks at Capri, lonely and lovely in the moonlight, the little shrines to the Madonna and Saints dotted in the most unexpected places throughout the city, the gold and pink majesty of Paestum at sunset, full-skirted petticoats on a street stall dancing a ballet as they got caught in a breeze, a little half-naked boy carrying a box of flowers on his head, then with a spurt of laughter I saw again a thin, under-nourished alley cat eating a plate of macaroni and sucking it up with the aplomb and dexterity of any Neapolitan gourmand. But there was less and less time for reminiscence. There were so many places I had yet to see and so many places I could not leave without a second visit. Cathleen accompanied me on farewell visits to Pompeii and Sorrento and to the lovely islands of Capri, Ischia and Prochida. I had to see again the glory of Monte Cassino's monastery on the mountain and scale a second time the heights of the 'Virgin's Mountain', where snowdrops and crocuses poked their heads through the snow drifts and a mysterious Russian madonna gazed serenely on the Italian pilgrims.

Every free moment was spent seeing more and more of this happy land and distilling experiences for the pot-pourri of memories. The Sisters, patients and all my friends had recommendations to make. 'You must see Caserta', and 'Sheila, you cannot leave without visiting Herculaneum'.

On one of our excursions we went to see Vesuvius. The view of the bay had always been dominated by the beautiful yet sinister mass of the volcano. We now wished to see it at closer quarters.

'It might warm your cold blood a little,' Lucia stated with a grin.

We took a 'bus which speeded quickly out of Naples to Pugliano where we changed to the special Vesuvius 'bus which wound its way up the tortuous roads affording breath-taking views of the country below. Everyone in the 'bus was extremely friendly, in the uninhibited and unselfconscious style of tourists.

We found ourselves sharing cable cars with two young men, one a Parisian, the other an Englishman. At the top we stepped out of our chair lift, shivering a little in the cool air – 4,000 feet higher than Naples. Then we were looking down into the stygian depth of this volcano which has had more than sixty eruptions. It was easy to visualize the terrible sight when, spitting molten flame, it erupted to completely bury two cities. Our two companions lacked the ability to create the mental picture and wished that it was still active.

'I wouldn't wish such terror and destruction on my worst enemy,' I stated, 'but if you really wish to see an active volcano, we have one in Naples.'

'Where?' they asked.

We explained that there was an active volcano at Sulfatara.

'Have dinner with us tonight?' they invited 'and then we'll go on an expedition to your volcano tomorrow.'

We agreed to have dinner, but explained to the pair that all our escorts had to be interviewed by Sister Patrick. They agreed, and at 8 p.m. sharp we saw from my window Jacques and Andrew appear.

They paled visibly when they saw Sister Patrick, like a Victorian Mama, formidably perched at the head of the stairs, but bravely came on to face the test. Luckily they passed with flying colours and Cathleen and I were soon immersed in our favourite roles as proud guides to our beloved city. Never did two guides have a more appreciative audience – the two men immediately fell in love with the lovely Naples by night, and the following day they showed a suitable degree of awed fascination at the heaving, bubbling, slimy-looking expanse of molten lava that was the volcano of Sulfatara.

Thus, as the sands of my time ran out, I continued to make new friends and became if possible, a more avid tourist than formerly.

Unfortunately we were constantly annoyed by would-be guides when we visited places of interest. Our difficulty was the fact that we could not afford to tip them. One could not say, rudely, 'Go away, we have no money'. We would say, 'No thanks, we do not require a guide'. They would ignore this protest and continue following us, droning, 'This is the actual bed in which Napoleon slept'. We would pretend not to understand. Undaunted, they switched to English, then French, followed rapidly by half a dozen other languages, gazing into our faces for our reaction to the language. We found it extremely difficult to look blank when we had understood. Finally we hit on the ruse of reciting 'The Lord's Prayer' in Gaelic until we shook off our followers.

We had managed to avoid the guides at Capodimonte, (formerly the Royal Palace and now the Naples Museum), and were enjoying the beautiful rooms and rare paintings, when, on entering a room, we found we were trapped. A young man in guide's uniform pounced on us ready to deliver his speeches.

'No thank you,' I said firmly, but when he

continued, I turned to him in exasperation and said a trifle rudely, 'Look here, please go away. We are only two poor students and we just can't *afford* a guide.'

'I don't mind in the least if you don't pay me,' be replied, 'I'm a student of English and doing this for the holidays and I *did* so want to 'show off' my English,' he added with disarming frankness. Mollified, we allowed him to guide us and we had to admit, the place was *much* more interesting when 'peopled' by this bright young man.

'Now this is the most beautiful room,' said the young student, as he threw open the doors of a magnificent ballroom with gleaming floor, sparkling mirrors and glistening chandeliers. He pressed a switch and the chandeliers sprang to life, shimmering sparkling diamonds of light which were reflected in the mirrors and floor. The whole room cried an invitation to the dance. I gazed at it longingly and so did the guide. Then suddenly, realizing that I too was wishing I could dance in that dream of a room, he asked impulsively, 'Will you dance?' Cathleen interposed nervously, 'Sheila, you shouldn't,' but I was already out on the floor being whirled expertly in a breathless tango, to which we supplied our own vocal music. We were really enjoying ourselves when the door opened and we were confronted by a cross-looking older guide who eyed us disapprovingly.

'The Signorina wished to dance,' our young man explained nervously.

Stern faced, the older one approached, bowed politely and with old world courtesy asked me for the next dance. Then before I knew what was happening I was engaged in a rather formal, old-time waltz. We danced stiffly the length of the room, where the old one, out of breath, bowed and thanked me, and I escaped with Cathleen before she turned purple trying to suppress her laughter.

Before the day came for me to leave, I had already forgotten my earlier tears and the struggle with the language, the torment I had undergone by the excessive heat of July and August, the misery of 'Italian tummy' and the inhospitable mosquitoes who shared me with their *parente* and left the natives of Italy alone. The things I knew I would remember forever, were the sunshine and glowing colour – not only of sky, flowers, fruit and scenery but colour of humanity, from the naked, brown-bottomed, sloe-eyed children with their wide grins, to the nobleman who, at the opera, described each forthcoming scene and songs with the detail of a connoisseur and the enthusiasm of a schoolboy; or how could I forget the street sweeper who had invited me, a stranger, into her humble home and not only shared a meal with me, but also her hopes, fears, aspirations and troubles. And that is what I loved about these people – that they were not merely open-handed to the foreigner, but open-hearted too.

What with all the packing, sight-seeing and shopping, the sunny days flew by until, incredibly, it was my last day on duty in Italy. Next day I would leave for Ireland, where there would be a grand reunion with my family. I looked forward immensely to seeing my parents, brothers and sisters again, yet I could not help feeling an unaccountable sadness for the family I was leaving behind. It was necessary to say goodbye to everyone from the director, Professor Caracciolo, to the staff and patients.

It was on the main hospital corridor that I met Caracciolo with his satellites, the three housemen, and approached to say goodbye. The old Professor thanked me warmly for my 'services to Italy', then, enveloping me in a bear's hug, he kissed me soundly. This demonstration was greeted with applause from the housemen causing Caracciolo to perform an encore. The many relatives who were as usual scouting around, loudly voiced their approval. By now the Professor's performance had gone to his head, and the size of the audience induced him to repeat the performance all over again. When I was finally released from the director's warm embraces and beheld the three housemen, grinning from ear to ear, as they bore down on me, preparing to play understudy to their star, I lost my nerve and, turning tail, fled. But there was more to come – all the nurses had to be kissed and promises were made to 'never forget' and 'write often'. I faced a still greater ordeal when I went to say good-bye to my patients. They were fond of me in that strange mixture of admiration and dependence which exists between patient and nurse; they were sorry that I was going, and being sad, they wept. This was quite unbearable for me, so that before long, in true Italian style, I too was in tears! Again it was Cathleen who rescued me from my slough of despondency.

'Wring out your handkerchief, Sheila,' she ordered, 'I prescribe a Mediterranean cruise and a large Marsala for your low spirits.'

I recovered nicely as we chugged around the bay in a motor boat for a 'panoramic tour' at 'lire two fifty'.

My heart nearly failed me again next day when it was time to say farewell to the nuns. They all crowded into my little room, as I had seen them do many times before – when I arrived in the beginning, after holidays, and at Christmas. They were all here again now – Sister Francis and the matron, Sister Patrick, who had been the first to welcome me at the station, Sister Jude (Dennis the Menace) and Sister Joan had come down from the theatre, and Claire and Teresa had forsaken their babies, Bernadette brought more messages from my ex-patients and the newest members of the community, Concepta and Margaret, added their voices to the goodbyes. The whole community was present when Sister Ann and Reverend Mother came in.

I was terribly lonely as I gazed around their dear, familiar faces – faces which betrayed tolerance and gentleness, charity and sacrifice, and shone with humour and perhaps, the too-lavish use of soap. They had received me, a stranger in their midst, and had from the very first day showered kindness and affection upon me. What a contradiction they were of the view that sanctity should be accompanied by long faces! The Sisters were always gay. As I thought of their patience and devotion to duty, coupled with their cheerful dispositions, I saw what leaving here would mean to me. Loving them because of, and not in spite of, their faults, I felt for them the same tolerant affection which one feels for one's own family.

My eyes stung as I said good-bye. As I swallowed the salt tears which ran down inside my throat, and with an effort composed myself to say farewell, I wished with all my heart for the childlike simplicity of the Neapolitan. I longed to be able to tell them how much I would miss them. The disciplined emotions and habits of years die hard, so it was a very formal good-bye which I managed to utter through stiff lips.

Perhaps they understood, though, in spite of my incoherence, for when the once formidable Sister Patrick clasped my hand to bid me farewell, she said, 'Come back to see us, won't you – *Sister?*'

The publishers hope that this book has given you enjoyable reading. Large Print Books are especially designed to be as easy to see and hold as possible. If you wish a complete list of our books please ask at your local library or write directly to:

Dales Large Print Books
Magna House, Long Preston,
Skipton, North Yorkshire.
BD23 4ND